AMANDA

GOES

TO

LAKTOSE

To Martha,

With My Best Wishes,

WOLFREN RIVERSTICK

First Edition

British Library Cataloguing in Publication Data
A catalogue recording for this book is available from the British Library

ISBN 978-0-9554314-2-5

Cover illustration by Michelle Martin of Willowmoor Art Workshop,
76 Crackley Bank, Chesterton, Newcastle-under-Lyme

Book design by Antony Rowe Ltd

Typeset by Crazy Wolf Books, Worcestershire, England
Published by Crazy Wolf Books
www.crazywolfbooks.com

Printed and bound in England by Antony Rowe Ltd,
Bumper's Farm, Chippenham, Wilts, SN14 6LH

For April, Joe and Daisy

CONTENTS

CHAPTER ONE

The School Essay

"Amanda... *AMANDA JAMES!*"

"Yes Mum?" said Amanda with a start, almost guiltily.

The whole classroom erupted into hysterical laughter upon hearing this. Meanwhile, Miss Ann Throwpee stared at Amanda with her customary tight-lipped expression which told her that she had said something quite ridiculous.

"What? Did I say something wrong?" asked Amanda in all innocence.

"You called her Mum!" whispered Amanda's best friend, Clare.

"Huh? Oh... whoops! Sorry Miss," Amanda apologised, her face quickly reddening as she snapped out of her daydream.

"Hmmph!" Miss Throwpee grunted. "Are you hard of hearing child or were you simply asleep?"

"Neither Miss, I... I..." stammered a rather embarrassed Amanda, but she could not think of a reasonable explanation.

"Never mind girl, I'll ask you the question again: why have you failed to hand in your essay on what you did during the summer holidays?"

"I haven't finished it yet Miss," Amanda promptly replied.

"Well, you've had two weeks to do it and everyone else has finished their work, so why should your story be any longer in content I ask you?"

"There's rather a lot to tell Miss, and I really don't know where to begin."

"So you haven't even started it then, is that what you're saying? It's just not good enough Amanda – I'll have to deduct you marks for this."

"Oh! But Miss, can't I have just a little more time please?" Amanda begged.

Although she was stern, Miss Throwpee was also fair. Having thought about Amanda's request for a moment or two she soon came back with her reply.

"Very well, but I want your work handed in by the end of the week and no later Amanda, or else you will be punished with detention during your break times."

"Thank you so much Miss Throwpee," said a relieved Amanda, breathing a sigh of relief.

The form teacher then turned her attention to the whole classroom.

"In the meantime children, whilst we wait with baited breath for Amanda James' epic novel…" she said, pausing briefly to glance disapprovingly over her spectacles at Amanda before continuing, "…I would like each of you to relate your summer adventures, reading your essays out loud to the rest of the class."

As usual, Miss Throwpee used her tried and trusted method of calling pupils in turn to read from the alphabetical order in which their names fell on the register. This meant that Terence Bull would be the first person to tell their story and Georgia Watts would be the last. Obviously, Amanda would not be called in turn because she had not finished her essay; therefore, she would now be the final member of the class to recall her summer holiday.

When summoned to stand before his classmates, Terence gave an amusing and highly interesting account of his family holiday in Greece. The former classroom bully was now a truly reformed character, having put his past as far behind him as he possibly could. Incidentally, it may be noted that he preferred to be called Terence nowadays, instead of the abbreviated version of his name, Terry, which he associated with his wild days.

Thus began the new autumn term at Sherbourne Hills Refectory School. It was just over a year since Amanda had moved to the village of Darwood, where she had settled in extremely well and made many new friends. A little less than two-hundred children in total attended Sherbourne Hills, with classrooms divided into groups of twenty pupils. Amanda was in Form VI and her teacher is – as has already been established – Miss Anne Throwpee. She would be Amanda's teacher for the duration of her schooling at Sherbourne Hills because, unlike most schools, the teacher moved up from year to year with their pupils whereas the norm would be to have a different form teacher each year.

This unusual teaching practice was employed because the school's governing body found that it allowed pupils to become more settled in their environment. Its proven method gave all of the children a chance to get to know their teacher; therefore the teacher could also become acquainted with his or her protégés. When the time eventually arrived for Amanda and her classmates to move on to finishing school, then Miss Throwpee would begin to teach her next batch of children for another term of office which would last for five years. Also, with this particular style of schooling, children looked upon their form teacher as a surrogate parent to whom they could come to and confide their innermost feelings or fears in the strictest of confidence.

Even though Miss Throwpee was a tough nut to crack, beneath her walnut shell exterior she was as soft as butter. In public she was the stereotypical matronly school ma'am but on a one-to-one basis she was a loving, caring individual whose warmth and kindness could melt the heart of a cabbage. Of course, all of the children in Form VI were aware of this and held her in the highest reverence.

Indeed, Miss Throwpee's bark was far worse than her bite; however, Amanda respected her immensely and she was determined to finish her essay by the end of the week so that she would not disappoint her teacher. So, for the next three nights Amanda wrote and wrote and wrote, working her fingers to the bone as she scribbled away with her favourite ballpoint pen. (It may be worth noting that pupils at Sherbourne Hills were encouraged to use their own handwriting rather than rely on a computer to produce their work.)

By the time Friday morning came around Amanda had written dozens of pages but her story was still nowhere near completion. And the reason that it was unfinished was because there just hadn't been enough time to put everything down on paper for, as she had told Miss Throwpee, there was so much to tell.

As usual, the morning lesson was late to commence after Miss Throwpee had made one of her feeble excuses and left the classroom. She returned ten minutes later reeking of stale tobacco smoke, which she tried to disguise with a mouthful of spearmint chewing gum. Then she cleared her throat. This was the warning system that told the children complete silence was now required. Instantly, law and order was restored to the classroom. The pupils sat quietly awaiting Miss Throwpee's bark whilst she peered ominously over the top of her spectacles until, eventually, her gaze focussed upon Amanda.

"Everyone has read their tales of summer adventures except for you Amanda; I do hope you're not going to disappoint us," grunted the teacher.

"No Miss, certainly not," Amanda replied politely.

"I'm glad to hear that," said Miss Throwpee, managing to raise a relieved smile. "Come up here then my child and read your story to the rest of the class."

Amanda took the unfinished essay from her bag and made her way to the front of the classroom.

"What on Earth have you got there? It looks like you really have written an epic novel!" said the surprised teacher when she espied the thick wad of paperwork in Amanda's hands.

"It's my essay Miss," Amanda proudly replied. "I did say that there was much to tell, so I thought I'd better start at the beginning."

"We'll be here all day by the looks of it!" grumbled the teacher. "Very well, the floor is yours. Make a start and we'll see how it goes from there," she continued, gesturing with her hand for Amanda to commence.

Amanda immediately began to relate her story, opening her account with the tale of when she moved from the big city to her new home in the countryside, and then describing the house she had moved into.

As she listened, Miss Throwpee scratched her head, at the same time pulling the most awful face.

"I thought I told you to write an essay about your summer adventures," she interrupted.

"Yes Miss, you did."

"Well, exactly what relevance does your move to this village last year have to do with this year's summer adventure?"

"Quite a lot actually Miss," Amanda explained. "In order for everyone to understand, it is necessary for me to establish the facts leading up to the summer."

Miss Throwpee looked a little bewildered but, nevertheless, she decided to give Amanda the benefit of the doubt.

"Carry on then," she surrendered, waving her hand nonchalantly in the air.

So, Amanda continued where she had left off, which was just about the point where she had explored the old barn in the garden of her parents' house. Then she introduced Skelly, Dave the milkman, Miss Peabody and her father Ted. She then mentioned all of the amazing adventures that she and her little alien friend Skelly had experienced together, although she left out some of the details that might embarrass Terence Bull, for she did not want to humiliate him now that he was a reformed character.

Finally, Amanda fondly related Skelly's grand send-off and his departure to the planet Laktose before closing her exercise book and looking up. The expression on her classmates' faces told her that they were totally enthralled with the tale, as they stared at her in disbelief. Even Miss Throwpee was unusually silent, sitting with her mouth agape whilst staring into space. Eventually she spoke.

"Is that it?" she asked.

"I haven't actually written any more but I still have the whole story to tell about what happened this summer," said Amanda apologetically, half expecting Miss Throwpee to be mad at her. But her teacher turned out to be far from angry.

"We've got all day, haven't we children?" she quickly said.

In reply, there was an appreciative and enthusiastic mumble of "Yes!" that uttered from every mouth in the classroom.

"Then it's unanimous... Do continue Amanda, it's an absolutely fascinating account," enthused Miss Throwpee.

"Huh? Oh... okay Miss," Amanda faltered. She had thought that her teacher would be annoyed because she had failed to write out the entire story, therefore she was somewhat taken aback by the response. So, immediately, without further hesitation, Amanda picked up the threads and willingly recommenced her tale.

And this is what she told them...

CHAPTER TWO

Boggles the Lab Rat

It had been many months since Skelly had returned to his home planet known as Laktose, situated in the far-away galaxy of the Milky Way, and Amanda missed him terribly. Not a single day had gone by when she had not thought about her dear little friend. She could clearly recall all of the fun times they had shared together in the brief period of time in which she had known him, and even the little mishaps that had befallen Skelly were imprinted firmly upon her mind. She now looked at these mishaps as fond memories because he had survived them all unscathed and even laughed about the events afterwards. How Amanda wished that she could see Skelly again – for just one more time, at least.

The winter months had dragged on and on, seeming to take an age to turn into spring. But when spring did eventually happen it was truly beautiful. Young shoots began to force their way through the ground surface as the first flowers began to appear; leaves slowly filled the bare branches of trees and they took on a whole new appearance; winter migrants returned to their roosts, chirruping merrily away as they settled down to start their new life for the next few months; and, best of all, temperatures slowly climbed to make the sunshine feel altogether warmer. Time passed a little quicker now, but Amanda still yearned to see Skelly.

Then came summer. It was the longest, hottest, driest season that Amanda had witnessed in all of her ten years. The days seemed much longer too because of the extra hours of daylight, although, in reality, they were the same length as they were at any time of the year. Summer holidays soon came around and Amanda found it hard to believe that it was a whole year since she and Skelly had been to the seaside together.

Amanda's mother, Janet, had recently landed a regular job at the village store, where she worked from nine o'clock in the morning until three o'clock in the afternoon, and her employment thus enabled her to be at home when Amanda returned from school. Mum only worked on Mondays, Tuesdays and Fridays, but this presented a slight problem during the holidays when Amanda was not at school. Fortunately, her father, Bill, was quite flexible with his working procedure and so it was decided that Amanda could spend certain days with him at the scientific laboratory where he worked. He realised that Amanda would not become bored because she had a keen interest in astronomy and he knew that he could find things to keep his daughter occupied, even if they were only small, unimportant tasks.

There was always plenty for Amanda to do at the laboratory – mainly cleaning jobs, ensuring all of the slides and test tubes were spotlessly clean, or polishing the work surfaces until she could see her reflection in them. She was not allowed to touch any of the lenses or telescopes though, because these were precision instruments that required sophisticated electronic equipment to remove the minutest particles of dust and fibre. Naturally, this equipment had to be operated by highly-skilled specialists, and Amanda was certainly not one of these qualified technicians so she was incapable of fulfilling the task.

The Laboratories for Interstellar Research were fortunate enough to possess one of the most powerful telescopes in the whole world, which was known as One-Eyed Jack, and sometimes Amanda's dad would let her take a peek at her favourite planet, Laktose. Over a short period of time Amanda learned all about the telescope until she became proficient in operating the device on her own. Once she was competent in all aspects of the telescope, she was allowed to use it unsupervised on every visit she made to the laboratories thereafter.

Because Laktose was in such a distant galaxy, most of the planet's entire surface appeared as a blur; nevertheless, Amanda studied it carefully, making notes and drawing diagrams as she did so. She used her imagination to invent details of what she thought the blurred areas would look like, trying to combine this with what she already knew about the planet from Skelly's past description. Not only that, but most of what she could see was shrouded in a fine, green, wispy veil of cloud anyway, so it really did not matter what her diagrams were like so long as they pleased her.

Very carefully, Amanda mapped the stars nearest to Laktose and all of the planets in our solar system in the order they appeared, starting from the Earth. The reason she did this was quite obvious – one day she hoped to go there! She did not know how she was going to achieve this goal but everyone has to have a dream, and this was Amanda's dream.

Amanda was alone at the laboratories for much of the time because her father was extremely busy that summer. This was due to the collapse of a large star which was sending asteroids hurtling through space at a frightening pace. Luckily, mankind was many light years away from the explosion so there was no danger of any fragments colliding with the Earth or any of its surrounding planets. However, a black hole had formed which was sucking the space debris towards it. Nobody knows too much about black holes, therefore the team of top scientists at the laboratories were watching this phenomenon avidly in an attempt to learn more about the event that was unfolding before their very eyes. This meant that One-Eyed Jack was now in constant use and Amanda could no longer study Laktose.

So, left to her own devices, she whiled away the time exploring the maze of rooms within the laboratories. Amanda had not set foot inside the vast chamber with the giant lasers since Skelly had been sent back to Laktose because it held such painful memories for her, but now that several months had passed she felt able to cope with her heartache and she decided to venture in. Once inside the huge chamber she fumbled around in the dark, searching for the banks of light switches until she located them. The rows of powerful spotlights took time to warm up, and in the dim lighting conditions Amanda could see the six giant lasers towering above her like silent robotic statues. Eventually, the spotlights reached their full capabilities, whereupon Amanda noticed that everything was just how she remembered it to be, with the massive glass skylight closed tightly shut and the small platform remaining in the centre of the room, still covered with a blue tarpaulin.

Amanda spun around and around, raising her head and watching the skylight whirling far above her, distant voices from the past echoing through her head as she recalled the party that had been arranged for Skelly's departure. For a few moments the sound of laughter filled the room, which mingled with the voices of her mum and dad, Dave the milkman, Ted Peabody and Skelly. Then there was that sombre quietness which had followed the event.

Amanda was deeply ensconced in this nostalgia trip until a tear suddenly rolled down her left cheek, which immediately brought the girl back to reality as she snapped out of her daydream. She had stopped spinning around too, and felt a giddy sensation in her head. After that a slight feeling of nausea briefly overcame her.

Wiping away the solitary tear, Amanda glanced at the centre stage before doing a double-take, because there was something beneath the tarpaulin which she had not noticed when she had first looked at it. Hurriedly, she grasped hold of the lightweight cover, at the same time tugging at the drawstrings that secured it, in order to loosen it off. Casting the tarpaulin to one side, Amanda gasped in complete amazement, for there on the platform in front of her was a space-egg just like the one that Skelly had travelled home in, although noticeably bigger. What was it doing there, she wondered? But before she could think any further about the matter a shadow loomed up in front of her, which almost made the young girl jump out of her skin.

"*Dad!*" Amanda exclaimed.

"I've been looking everywhere for you," said her father. "This is the last place I expected to find you... I see you've discovered our space-egg."

"Where did you get it?" asked Amanda.

"We built it ourselves. It's an exact replica of Skelly's space-egg except that it's built on a slightly larger scale – big enough to convey a human being," Dad proudly announced.

"But how did you manage to copy it?"

"Ah, there's quite a simple explanation really," Dad told her. "You see, when Skelly's original space-egg was here we scanned every single aspect – inside and out – on a three-dimensional scale."

"How clever," Amanda remarked.

"We have the technology," Amanda's father added, rather triumphantly.

"Does it work? I mean, will it fly into space?"

"We certainly hope so, although that remains to be seen. There are a few adjustments yet to be made, but we're getting there. A lot of money has been invested in this machine, together with countless hours of time and effort, so we daren't send her on a maiden voyage until we're absolutely sure."

"How will you know when it's ready to fly?" Amanda asked excitedly, new thoughts suddenly rattling around within her brain.

"We'll know," Dad replied enthusiastically, and then he gestured towards the door. "Come with me... I've got something else to show you."

Amanda's father led her along the corridor to the very rear of the research complex until they reached a solid steel door, secured by a combination lock and three high-tensile steel padlocks. He took a bunch of keys out of his pocket and unlocked the padlocks one at a time. Following this procedure, he turned the combination lock until it clicked loudly, before putting all of his weight against it and heaving the door open.

The room behind the secure door contained several large steel-mesh cages, stacked high to the ceiling, most of which appeared to be empty. An animal scent, unfamiliar to Amanda, lingered in the air, merging with a strong odour of disinfectant. At the far end of the room, nearest the window, Amanda noticed some movement in one of the cages. Together, she and her father approached the cage, whereupon Dad released the latch. He reached inside and rummaged around amongst the mass of wood-shavings and straw until he finally pulled out a large, white rodent. Holding the creature slightly aloft, while at the same time stroking it gently behind the ears, Dad turned to face Amanda with a huge smile on his face.

"This is our lab rat, Boggles," he told her. "He's quite a character you know."

Amanda stared at the rat in awe. She had never seen one so closely before and had not realised that they could be quite so large.

"Do you want to hold him?" asked Dad.

"I'm not really sure," gasped Amanda. "Does he bite?"

Dad laughed at this.

"No, he's perfectly harmless, as well as being fully house-trained and extremely intelligent."

"He smells a bit though, doesn't he?" remarked Amanda, wrinkling up her nose.

"All animals do – even humans… Here, take hold of him, I think he likes you."

Rather reluctantly, Amanda accepted Boggles in her arms. His sleepy, red, beady eyes darted about as he focused upon her, all the while his nose twitching busily as he sniffed this odour that was new to him. Boggles' long whiskers tickled Amanda's skin as he swished them to and fro during his brief but frantic investigation of her. Then he settled down, nestling snugly into the crook of the girl's arms. Amanda had grown to like him already.

"Ah, he's so adorable… Who's a little cutie then?" she muttered in a soft voice.

"Yes, isn't he?" Dad agreed. "And, I'll bet you didn't know that rats are considered to be filthy creatures and yet, in reality, they are one of the cleanest animals on the planet."

"No, I didn't know!" Amanda said, seeming surprised.

"Let's put him back in his cage now," said Dad. "You can feed him if you want to and give him some fresh water also – he's very partial to the odd carrot or two. In fact, you can feed him every time that you visit the laboratories in future… because I think he has definitely taken a liking to you."

Amanda was overjoyed at this suggestion and she willingly agreed.

"What's in the other cages?" she asked as her father locked Boggles' cage door.

"They contain rats too. They're Boggles' companions but their characters aren't as strong as his. We selected him for that very reason."

"Selected him for what?"

"He's our test pilot. You see, we have also built a miniature space-egg – another replica but on a much smaller scale. It's our prototype from which we shall learn and then refine the real one if necessary."

Amanda was horrified.

"You're going to send Boggles into space?" she said questioningly.

"Yes, very soon... next week, in fact. He's been up there twice already, so he's an old hand at it now. You'll have to come along and watch the launch."

For the next few moments they worked in silence as Dad showed Amanda how to feed and water Boggles the lab rat, and then they departed. As they left the room Amanda's father secured the steel door behind them.

"I've noticed that there are an awful lot of locks on this door Dad," Amanda commented, "...more than there are on the doors of the rooms which contain really expensive equipment."

Her father sighed loudly.

"Sadly, it's a sign of the times," he said, with a serious expression on his face. "We need the locks in case of an invasion by animal rights activists. They think that all laboratories treat animals badly; that we are inhumane and do terrible experiments to the creatures. Unfortunately, for humans to develop it is necessary to use animals for testing purposes because there would be much more of an outcry if we sacrificed human lives."

"Do you do terrible things to animals?" asked Amanda.

"Of course not!" Dad retorted rather indignantly. "All of our testing is carried out in the most caring manner. We only keep a handful of rats here – nothing else – and they are treated like kings."

"I thought so," Amanda said, and she paused before adding her next sentence. "I've decided that I would like to come along next week to watch the launch of the space-egg."

"Good, I am pleased. It will be an interesting experience for you," her father said, beaming at her. Then he changed the subject. "It's time to go home now. Get your bag from the staff room and meet me in the lobby in five minutes."

Amanda was deep in thought as they walked to the car.

"Boggles is a funny name for a rat," she said at length.

"Well, Biggles is the name of a famous pilot in a series of novels written by the author Captain W. E. Johns – I believe the character's name was Bigglesworth actually, but I can't be sure. Anyway, I thought it was an appropriate name for the rat because he too is a bit of a pilot. Not only that, but he seems a little confused at times – as if things are quite mind-boggling – so the name seems to fit him perfectly."

"Yes, Boggles suits him just fine," agreed Amanda.

"Fancy a pizza for tea?" asked Dad. "We can stop at your favourite place, Pizzas of Eight, on the way home and pick one up if you like."

"What a great idea," Amanda said, her voice full of excitement. "We can have the perfect topping for what has been a perfect day."

CHAPTER THREE

Lost in Space

During the following week Amanda was given the responsibility of caring for Boggles. Every day, at the same time, she fed the rat and then took him out of his cage to put him through his daily exercise routine. Boggles was under a strict training programme to ensure that he was in peak physical condition for his space voyage and a special run had been constructed specifically for this purpose. This incorporated a series of obstacles, wheels, hurdles and even a tiny treadmill, the whole circuit being affectionately dubbed as 'The Rat Race'.

Eventually, the time came for Boggles to be launched into space. All of the scientists at the research establishment assembled in the Room of Interstellar Activity, taking their places ready for the great event. Obviously, Boggles could not really operate the controls of the miniature space-egg; nor was he expected to because it was electronically controlled from the command centre. The sole purpose of Boggles' existence in the space-egg was actually to test whether it was possible to survive for up to a week in the tiny capsule, for that was how long the scientists had estimated it would take to travel to the planet known as Laktose. Amanda was sad to see Boggles depart because she had grown quite attached to him.

"He'll be back," Amanda's father reassured her as Boggles was duly placed into the small cockpit and the canopy snapped tightly shut, automatically creating an air-tight seal. Then the capsule was pressurised and the massive glass skylight began to slowly open. Meanwhile, the six giant lasers swung into place and began to power-up; however, due to the minute size of the space-egg, a much smaller amount of radiation would be required than was applied when Skelly had previously been launched from that very room.

All of the preliminary checks were carried out before the launch to ensure that everything was in order and, once they were satisfied with their results, the scientists gave the thumbs-up sign and a nod of approval. The space-egg, and Boggles the rat, were now ready for a third trip into orbit.

When the lasers had reached their required level of power there was a sudden blinding flash of light, followed by a loud whooshing sound, and it was all over in an instant – the space-egg had disappeared from the platform. There was a loud cheer from the scientists as they gawped upwards, watching the tiny dot of light disappearing into the atmosphere until it was no more.

After that everyone removed their dark eye goggles, which had been necessary to protect their eyes from the glare of the laser arc, before settling down to observe the flight on their personal monitors. Cameras were immediately switched on in sequence when signals were rebounded off strategically placed satellites as the space-egg sped past each one in turn. And, from a microscopic camera installed in the cockpit of the space-egg, it was possible to view the interior where Boggles could clearly be seen, busily chomping away at a piece of carrot, completely unaware of the importance that this space voyage signified to mankind.

For the first three days the flight went smoothly but then things unexpectedly began to go horribly wrong.

"Uh-oh, we have developed a problem!" one of the scientists announced out of the blue.

The remaining members of the scientific crew immediately crammed around his monitor so they too could take a look at the problem which had just arisen.

"The space-egg has left its guided route and I can't get it back on course," the scientist told them.

"It could be a fault with your programme... Let me see if I can correct its course using my computer controls," said another scientist, whose name was Ben.

But although the man tried hard to put things right, he could not get the space-egg to follow its designated path. At this point, Amanda's father intervened. He was now seated back at the master controls and he instantly switched on the giant overhead monitor so that everyone could view the predicament together without having to crowd around a small computer screen.

"I think I know what the problem is," he quickly announced. "The force from the black hole is extremely strong – much more powerful than we anticipated – therefore the space-egg can't avoid its pull because it's too light to contend with it."

"What do you suggest we do then Bill?" asked Mike, the scientist who had initially spotted that there was a problem.

"We shall have to switch on the rocket boosters to override the space-egg's power controller, Mike."

"Yes, maybe that will work," agreed Ben, whose responsibility it would be to carry out this task. "The enormous power thrust should, in theory, realign it – although it may well drain the main power circuit."

"We have little choice," Amanda's dad concluded. "You have my authority to go ahead with the operation... *Immediately!*"

Ben hurriedly pressed several buttons on his console and waited patiently for a response, but nothing happened.

"It's not working," he said in disappointment. "The after-burners just won't fire!"

"The power-shift has failed also," added Mike.

"Darn it! There must have been an electrical arc that has caused a short in the power supplies," muttered Amanda's father. "Switch to auxiliary power Ben."

Ben responded to his request but that would not work either.

"It's hopeless," Ben said. "We're lost!"

"We're not lost, but the space-egg will be if we can't do anything," Amanda's father replied.

But there was nothing that could be done and the team of scientists watched helplessly as the space-egg drifted closer to the black hole. At that moment Amanda walked into the room. She had been tending to Boggles' companions and had therefore missed the conversation between the scientists. Having sensed the gloomy atmosphere within the control room, it did not take her long to realise that something was amiss. Then, when she stared at the giant monitor, she noticed the enormous swirling mass of blackness that was drawing the tiny space-egg ever nearer.

"What going to happen to Boggles?" Amanda cried.

Nobody answered her.

"You told me that he'd be back..." she continued, turning towards her father.

"Quiet, Amanda! This is not the time to become emotional. We're concentrating," her father shouted. His voice had become agitated and Amanda recognised this, so she immediately hushed up.

"Switch to the cockpit camera. We can at least record what the dashboard dials are doing," he demanded.

The interior camera was immediately switched on. All that could be seen though, were two large, beady, red eyes and a spray of moving whiskers as Boggles sniffed at the camera lens.

"I don't believe it! The flippin' rat's in the way... Try the in-flight camera instead," snapped Amanda's dad.

When this was turned on, a superb view of the mouth of the black hole could instantly be seen.

"This is history in the making," uttered Ben. "At least we can salvage something out of the mission... this is the first-ever bird's-eye view of a black hole."

"Shouldn't that be a rat's-eye view?" asked Mike, but his attempt at a joke was not appreciated.

All of a sudden every single camera simultaneously went blank when the space-egg began to enter the black hole. With nothing left but radar contact, there followed a sombre silence as everyone in the Room of Interstellar Activity watched the blip on the radar screen become fainter until it finally disappeared altogether.

Without getting up, Amanda's father pushed his swivel-chair away from his console and, placing his hands behind his head, he sank back into his seat.

"It's all over," he said. "Abort the mission gentlemen… let's wrap it up."

The scientists knew exactly what he meant by this remark. In complete silence they went about the business of shutting down the banks of electrical equipment which had been monitoring the space-egg. No leads were to be unplugged though, because it would be necessary to find out exactly what had caused the malfunction which had put paid to the mission.

Exactly one hour later Amanda found herself travelling home in the car with her father, and she was extremely upset by the day's events.

"Cheer up sweetheart," said Dad. "It's not the end of the world."

This was the longest sentence he had said to her since the space mission had been aborted.

"I'm concerned about Boggles. What will happen to him now Dad?" sobbed a heartbroken Amanda.

"I don't know love… I really don't know. I'm sure he will be okay though," he replied in an attempt to comfort her. "In the meantime, I shall have to find a way of explaining to my superiors – as well as our American sponsors – about the loss of their multi-million dollar space-egg."

"I don't care about their stupid space-egg…" Amanda began, but she was interrupted by her father before she could finish.

"I know it doesn't mean anything to you, but it means an awful lot to me. If I don't come up with a reasonable explanation for the loss, then our space programme will be halted and I won't be able to get another sponsor. That will mean that my research at the laboratory will have to come to an end, and all of the scientists will have to look for another job – including me!"

"I thought you told me that your research laboratories didn't harm animals," Amanda continued relentlessly.

"That's enough Amanda!" snapped her father. He was at the end of his tether and was obviously under considerable stress.

"But you have always taught me that life was more important than material things. Surely that includes animals too?"

Dad remained quiet for a few moments whilst he collected his thoughts.

"You're quite right," he said at length. "Unfortunately though, things don't always go as planned. Sometimes there have to be sacrifices in the name of research, and in this case it was an animal. If it had been a human being, imagine how their family would be feeling right now. I really do care about the loss of Boggles, but tragedy is a fact of life and something that we have to learn to live with."

Amanda had no choice but to accept this explanation and the remainder of the journey was spent in silence.

It was not until two days later that the reason for the loss of the space-egg was finally discovered. Apparently, a simple blob of solder on one of the silicon chips had been omitted, therefore the electrical circuit could not be completed. This meant that (as Amanda's father had said at the time) an arc had caused an electrical short-out that had brought about the demise of the space-egg.

The full-size space-egg was then checked over and the same fault was also found. It was thus rectified to prevent the same mishap occurring. The sponsors of the space mission were informed about the results of the findings and they subsequently agreed to continue with the programme. As far as the scientists were concerned, the full-size machine was now ready for its maiden flight. It was at this point that Amanda began to hatch a plan.

CHAPTER FOUR

Blast Off!

A shrill bleeping sound awoke Amanda with a start. It was one of those alarm tones that got louder the longer it was left to run and it sounded as if a huge truck was reversing inside her bedroom. Amanda jumped out of bed, staggered across the bedroom in a sleepy haze and slammed her hand down hard onto a button that was situated on top of her alarm clock. It immediately went quiet. Then she yawned and stretched her limbs before ambling back across the bedroom floor to crawl beneath the warm bedclothes again. She hated getting up early, especially when she didn't have to go to school, so there was no reason for her to set the alarm clock... or was there?

Suddenly she opened her eyes wide as she remembered why the alarm had gone off. Today was a big day for her. As quick as could be, she leapt from her bed once more and began to rummage through her cupboard drawers, selecting only the bare necessities for her trip. She knew she would have to travel light because, for one thing, there was not enough room, and, for another, she did not want to draw attention to herself.

Amanda proceeded to fill her backpack with lightweight clothes, a torch, half-a-dozen disposable cameras and a hairbrush. Then she picked up her favourite teddy bear and stuffed that in as well – Brumus the bear always travelled with her when she went on a long journey. A quick peek inside her bag revealed that there was just enough space left to stock up with a few items of food. Hastily, she picked up the backpack and threw it onto the bed. There followed a pitiful squawk from Tabs as the laden bag landed right in the very spot where the cat had been curled up fast asleep.

"You poor thing!" whispered Amanda as she picked up the frightened animal, hugging her close to her heart whilst she apologised. "Sorry Tabs, I didn't mean to startle you."

She scooped up the distraught cat in her arms and kissed Tabs on top of her head, just behind the ears, before placing her gently back onto the bed in the hollow that had formed where she had previously lay. But Tabs immediately got up again and made a swift exit from the bed before shooting out of the bedroom door as fast as a rocket.

Amanda picked up her backpack and left the bedroom also. She peered anxiously along the landing and was pleased to find that there was no sign of her mum and dad yet. They must still be asleep, she thought. On tiptoes she crept quietly downstairs, purposely avoiding the ones that creaked, and into the kitchen. Then she raided the cupboards, taking as much food as she possibly could until she could get no more into the backpack.

When this was done Amanda stepped out into the garden. Dawn had not long broken: the birds were beginning to twitter as they broke into their early morning chorus, the sun was just starting to peep cheerfully over the hillside, and the sky was an awesome shade of blood red on the horizon. It looked as if it was going to be a beautiful day.

Skipping merrily along the garden path as she went, the girl then set off towards the former tumbledown barn that had now been transformed into a small stable block, for the time had come to say goodbye to Milkstar. When she got there, it was obvious that the magnificent pure white mare was pleased to see the girl, although she did appear to be surprised to see her owner quite so early in the morning. Amanda always visited Milkstar before breakfast, solely for the purpose of feeding the animal, but today she thought that she would get there at the crack of dawn in order to take Milkstar for a short ride before departing on her trip, because it would be some time before she got the chance to do so again.

After quickly saddling-up, she led Milkstar through the garden gate into a neighbouring field. There were several acres of land here that a local farmer let Amanda use so long as she kept to the perimeter of the fields or to marked bridlepaths. Amanda mounted her steed and rode off into the sunrise, setting off at a fast trot, although she slowed to a leisurely pace for the most part. She returned home one hour later, feeling thoroughly exhilarated by the early morning experience. Of course, Milkstar had enjoyed the ride too and she would benefit from the exercise immensely because Amanda had not found much time for riding of late.

Before returning Milkstar to her stable, Amanda brushed the horse's shiny coat and gave her a huge hug, patting and stroking her muscular neck whilst she did so. It was hard to say goodbye because she loved her horse dearly and knew that she would miss the animal greatly while she was away.

After that she walked along the garden path to return to the house. Tabs ran to greet her, meeting her halfway, her bushy tail flapping lazily around Amanda's ankles as she purred and meowed noisily. The astute cat had sensed that something was happening. Amanda picked up her faithful pet and hugged her tightly.

"I'll miss you too Tabs," she said, "but I'll be back soon, so don't worry."

Mum and Dad were already at the breakfast table when Amanda entered through the kitchen door.

"You must have been up with the lark this morning," was her mother's greeting. "Did you enjoy your ride?"

"Yes, thanks," Amanda politely replied.

"You timed your return perfectly," said Mum. "Breakfast is on the table."

Amanda had worked up a huge appetite and she ate a hearty breakfast of bacon, egg, sausage and beans. After she had eaten Amanda got up from the table and threw her arms around her mother, giving her the biggest hug she had ever had and clinging firmly to her as if she could not let go.

"You're only going to work with your father," laughed Mum. "Anyone would think I wasn't going to see you for a while! I'll see you later darling."

"Yes," Amanda said, but that was all she could find to say. She picked up her backpack, placed it in Dad's car and off they went to the laboratories.

Amanda poked her head around the door in the Room of Interstellar Activity to find that the coast was clear. It appeared that the scientists, who had spent most of the morning setting up the full-size space-egg ready for its launch, had now gone for a lunch break. At two-thirty that afternoon the space-egg was due to be sent into space for its maiden voyage and Amanda was ready to go with it.

When the girl was absolutely sure that there was nobody else in the room, she dashed across the floor to the launch platform. She opened the canopy, bundled her backpack into the cockpit and then climbed into the space-egg, pulling the canopy shut behind her. Then she waited patiently, safe in the knowledge that nobody would be able to see her through the black smoked glass of the cockpit, although she could see out of it. At a quarter-to-two Amanda's father and his team of scientists returned to the Room of Interstellar Activity and began the launch sequence.

"Hold it!" shouted one of the scientists just before the countdown was about to start. "There's a warning light flashing on my monitor informing me that the canopy isn't secured."

"That's odd!" said Amanda's father, with a puzzled frown on his face. "I shut the canopy myself and the fault didn't show up when we carried out the preliminary checks this morning."

Having made this remark, he walked over to the space-egg and locked the clasps that held the canopy in place, without making any inspection whatsoever.

"There!" he said triumphantly. "That ought to do it."

With this done, he returned to the master controls, never giving a second thought as to the reason why the canopy had mysteriously become unlocked. Then the countdown began with no further hindrances. During this time the scientists prepared themselves for the unmanned space launch, totally unaware that the space-egg actually contained a passenger.

"...FIVE, FOUR, THREE, TWO, ONE..." came the sound of the automated voice as the countdown sequence finalised.

"...ZERO...WE HAVE LIFT-OFF!"

The space-egg soared high into the clear, blue afternoon sky, once again to the sound of a loud unanimous cheer from the occupants of the control room, just as they had done on the day of Skelly's departure all those months ago. Amanda could hear the automated countdown voice through the speakers within the cockpit of the space-egg. She also heard the deafening cheer of delight too, and she had waited with baited breath when it was discovered that the cockpit canopy was not secured, breathing a huge sigh of relief when she realised that she was not going to be found out.

Having closed her eyes tightly shut for the duration of the lift-off, Amanda now opened them again – very slowly. In just those few brief seconds the space-egg had already travelled high into the atmosphere. From there, the view of the Earth appeared in a blue haze but the oceans and landmasses were still clearly to be seen; however, Amanda's home planet was becoming smaller all of the while as it got left further behind. The space-egg continued to accelerate until it reached its orbital velocity – this was the thrust needed for it to reach its orbit – at which point it then stayed in orbit around the Earth until it had achieved a complete lap of its circumference. Once the scientists were sure that everything was functioning properly, they fired the booster rockets that supplied the escape velocity which would take the capsule into deep space.

Since launching the space-egg there had been complete silence in the capsule, but this was suddenly interrupted by the sound of a voice. At the same time, a television screen flickered to life in front of Amanda.

"I think you ought to take a look at this Bill..." said the voice.

At that moment the television screen became clear and Amanda could see the looks of astonishment on the faces of the team of scientists. Then her father appeared in the midst of them, the joyous expression on his face turning to a look of horror when he realised what he was seeing.

"*AMANDA!*" exclaimed Dad.

"Hi Dad," Amanda replied nonchalantly.

"Is this some sort of prank? How did you get up there?"

"Why, you launched me from your research laboratories," Amanda wilfully replied.

"This is not a laughing matter Amanda – we shall now have to bring you back to Earth immediately. The whole mission is ruined... *again!*"

"It's not ruined," one of the scientists intervened. "In fact, it's been a complete success because we have proved that the full-size space-egg works and that a human being can survive in it."

"Hmmph! I agree with you Alf, but we still have to bring the vessel back to Earth."

"I'm not coming back yet," said Amanda.

"Oh, yes you are, young lady... You have no choice! We're bringing you back right now," her father told her.

"No, you're not, Dad!" Amanda defiantly retorted, and she instantly switched the controls to manual override.

"We've lost control of the space-egg," said Ben.

"*AMANDA!*"

"Don't panic, Dad, I know how to fly this thing. I've been reading the manual and I've learned all about it. Now I'm going to find Skelly."

"*You're going to find Skelly?*" chorused the team of scientists in surprise.

"Yes, I'm going to visit Skelly," Amanda proudly replied.

"Well, it appears that you've made up your mind," said Dad, "and, as you are no longer within our control, I need to explain something to you… Listen carefully Amanda."

"I'm listening, Dad."

"The space-egg is not just a state-of-the-art spacecraft… It also has the capability of travelling through time."

"Cool!" said Amanda.

"There is a large green button on the dashboard to the left of you that has the word 'Hyperspace' printed on it. Do you see it Amanda?"

"Yes, I see it."

"Press this button only when necessary – It will allow you to get out of trouble. For instance, if there is an approaching meteor storm you can avoid it because the button will enable you to jump to another time in space. It may be possible to jump several light years at a time, but we're not absolutely sure about that."

"I'll figure it out," said Amanda. "I'm not stupid… I know how to play computer games."

There was a roar of laughter from the scientists in the control room upon hearing this, but they soon fell silent when their team leader glared at them.

"This is the real thing Amanda; it's not a game," said Dad in a grave voice.

"I know," Amanda wearily replied.

"And another point of prime importance," continued her father, "is that you should always keep the horizon viewfinder horizontal – that's the dial in front of you which is shaped like a ball and rolls about a bit – otherwise you will be flying upside down and will eventually crash into something."

"I've already worked that out," said Amanda. "It's quite simple really; all you have to do is twist the joystick and steer it one way or the other."

"Well, being as you are so conversant with the space-egg controls already, there's obviously nothing else I need to tell you," Amanda's father said rather indignantly.

"I'll be fine Dad, honest I will. Please don't worry about me."

"It's not so much you that I'm worried about – it's your mother who concerns me the most… I don't know what she'll do when she finds out. I haven't a clue what I am going to tell her."

"I'm sure you'll think of something Dad – you usually do."

"What's it like to travel through space Amanda?" asked her father. "I've often wondered."

"Really cool!" replied Amanda excitedly. "It's dead quiet, peaceful, and quite dark really."

"There's an in-flight camera mounted on the fuselage Amanda, make sure that you take some decent pictures for me, won't you?"

"Yes Dad," said Amanda, laughing.

"We've lost visual contact now," Ben interrupted.

"We'll be losing sound contact with you as well soon Amanda because you'll be out of communications range," her father warned her. "Take good care of yourself and have a safe journey."

"Thanks Dad... I love you."

"I love you too, sweetheart."

Before Amanda's father could say anything else the speakers fizzled out to leave nothing but a dull buzzing noise.

"You must be very proud of your daughter," said Mike. "She's making history today, you know, because she's the first child in space – *ever!*"

"Yes, I do know," Amanda's father said mournfully, "but I can't help worrying about her all the same."

"As a parent myself, that's a natural reaction of course," Mike said as he tried to console him. "She appears to be an intelligent child to me though, so I'm sure she'll be fine if she keeps her wits about her... Your daughter appears to know what she's doing."

"Yes, I'm sure that she knows exactly what she's doing! However, I have to remind myself that Amanda is only ten years old. Mind you, she has always been quite advanced for her years: she was quite an outstanding reader by the time she was just five and mathematics comes naturally to her, but she is still a mere child nonetheless. All I can do now is hope and pray that she will be alright."

"We'll all be praying," echoed Mike, Ben and Alf, all at the same time.

Amanda's father nodded his appreciation of his team-mates' support, and then he changed the subject.

"Right, let's shut everything down and go home," he said. "There's nothing further that we can do for the present."

CHAPTER FIVE

The Milky Way

Once Amanda had lost contact with the control centre she was on her own. When she glanced in her retractable rear-view mirrors, the Earth was just a tiny speck in the distance – if, indeed, it was the Earth at all. Actually, every single planet now looked the same to her. The view to the front and sides was much the same: nothing but a maze of stars, all of a similar likeness. And there really was not much for Amanda to do because her father had preset the co-ordinates of the space-egg (just as he had done when he sent Skelly back to Laktose), so she restored the controls of the space-egg to auto-pilot, reclined her seat and fell asleep.

A short while later Amanda awoke and immediately began to panic as she wondered where she was. However, she soon recalled that she was on her space voyage and quickly relaxed. There is no real concept of time in space, but, at that precise moment, Amanda glanced at her watch anyway, purely out of habit. She noticed that its hands were going haywire; so, because she found this irritating, she took off her timepiece and tucked it safely away in her backpack. Then she opened a packet of chocolate biscuits because she felt a little peckish.

All of a sudden, Amanda became aware of the fact that the space-egg was travelling faster than it had been before she fell asleep. Trying not to panic, she grabbed the controls, reverting to manual override again so that she was now in full control of the vessel, but the space-egg would not respond. Ahead of her Amanda could see a huge, swirling void of black where no stars apparently existed, which was constantly growing larger. And the reason why the dark mass was getting bigger was because it was becoming closer. Little did she know that the space-egg was being sucked into a black hole and there was nothing that could be done to prevent this from happening.

In no time at all Amanda and the space-egg were surrounded in complete darkness as they entered the mouth of the black hole. Before she had embarked on her space voyage Amanda had read all that she could find out about black holes, learning that there was supposed to be no way out of one. As far as she knew, they swallowed everything in their path and nothing ever escaped because of their incredible force; therefore, when she finally realised what was happening, she had no clue what could be done about it.

Just as the girl began to be thrown violently from one side of the capsule to the other, she remembered what her father had told her about the green Hyperspace button on the dashboard of the space-egg. Without any hesitation whatsoever, she reached for the button and pressed it firmly – not once, but five times in total. Then she fastened her safety belt and waited to see what would happen.

She didn't have to wait long either, because, in the space of a mere nanosecond, her vision suddenly became distorted. After that there was a flash of bright light, followed by distortion again. At the same instance, Amanda's cheeks wobbled and shook, pulling her face painfully in every direction possible as the capsule rocketed her through dimensions of space at an incalculable speed, previously unknown to mankind. Eventually though, things settled down again and her vision returned to normal.

With calm restored, it appeared that the space-egg was now drifting slowly amongst a huge cluster of planets. As far as she could see in every direction there were millions of them. No, in fact, there were billions of stars, mostly shrouded in a thin veil of mist. There were so many planets in such close proximity that Amanda realised she had ended up slap-bang in the centre of the Milky Way. Somehow or other, maybe due to sheer luck, it seemed that Amanda had been transported through time and had arrived at her destination.

But it was not just sheer luck that had brought her here, because her father had actually been instrumental in getting her to her target. He had input the precise co-ordinates into the computer and, when Amanda had operated the Hyperspace button, the time machine had jumped 25,000 light years in one swoop! You see, each touch of the button was equal to a leap of 5,000 light years and Amanda had pressed it five times, which meant that she had arrived at the Milky Way in just a split-second of time in human terms. This turned out to be the only bit of luck involved.

At this point of her journey though, Amanda was faced with another dilemma: namely, which planet was Laktose? She removed a wad of paperwork from her backpack and scoured the numerous maps and diagrams but she could not make head or tail of them. It looked totally different from this angle now

45

that she was amongst the one-hundred-billion or so stars that made up the Milky Way. Amanda felt totally overawed, but there was no need for concern because her clever father came to the rescue once again. His co-ordinates were so exact that, very soon, the space-egg began to descend towards a large, bright planet, covered with a fine green mist.

As she entered the outer atmosphere of the planet Amanda braced herself for the bumpy ride ahead. It was just like being in a jet plane when it enters cloud cover, she thought, because the turbulence threw her around like a rag doll, making it seem as if it would never end. But, in no time at all, the thick cloud thinned-out and everything felt smooth again. Amanda squinted her eyes, for, at exactly the same moment, she had emerged into daylight. After travelling for so long in the darkness that had existed throughout space it took a few seconds for her eyes to readjust, but she blinked repeatedly and rubbed her eyes until she was able to focus. Then she could not believe what was happening because, somehow or other, the space-egg was flying upside down.

Amanda twisted the joystick until the space-egg had rotated the correct way up, so that the blue sky was above her and the green pastures of the ground were below her. But something was not quite right, for the horizon viewfinder told her that she was still the wrong way up! That was impossible though, because, according to the flight manual, the viewfinder was supposed to be one-hundred per cent accurate. So she readjusted the steering controls again and, at the very moment that she did so, there was a whooshing sound and a huge jolt which made the girl jump in fright. Trembling a little, she hesitantly peered out of the glass cockpit, only to find that two large parachutes had been released to act as drag chutes that would slow down the descent of the capsule.

In theory, this now meant that she had to be falling towards the ground. However, the altimeter showed that the space-egg was losing height although, confusingly, the ground was blue and the sky was green! Amanda checked the horizon viewfinder once more, to discover that it was working perfectly, and she felt totally baffled.

But, before she had time to think about it any further, the space-egg touched down on the surface of the planet, bouncing several times as it skimmed across the land like a flat stone skims on water. Finally it came to rest, its impact cushioned by the thick blue grass that surrounded it.

Amanda was totally astonished to learn that the reason for her confusion was quite simple: of course, the sky was green and the grass was blue – the exact opposite of how it was back on Earth! She was also amazed that she had survived her space voyage unscathed and was now the first person *ever* to land on a planet other than the moon. Then she began to feel frightened as she wondered what to do next. Lots of questions went through her mind: where would she go now that she had landed? What would she do? Would it be safe to step into the atmosphere of the planet Laktose? This was what currently concerned her more than anything.

Following a careful study of the vessel's atmosmeter and, after checking the recommended levels of oxygen in the space-egg manual, Amanda was satisfied that the levels were exactly the same as they were on Earth. It also dawned on her that

Skelly had survived for many years on her planet; therefore the air on Laktose must be suitable for her.

But how was she to get out of the capsule, she asked herself? Her father had locked the canopy in place, so she imagined that there must be an escape hatch – or something like that, at least. Search as she may though, Amanda failed to find an alternative means of exit, and she resorted to consulting the manual once more. According to its instructions, there was a lever beneath the pilot's seat that operated an ejector seat, so Amanda fumbled around until she found it. She tugged and pulled at the lever all to no avail, and it was only when she pushed the button on the tip of the lever that it finally decided to work. Instantly, there was a dull thud, closely followed by another one.

CLUNK! CLUNK!

The outer locks of the canopy became unclasped and then the canopy slid sideways. This was followed by a loud hiss of air.

WHOOSH!

Without any further warning Amanda and her seat were suddenly airborne. But, what goes up must come down, and just when she began to question what was going to prevent her from ploughing into the ground, a miniature parachute opened up and Amanda floated slowly down. Following this, she breathed an immediate sigh of relief, and then several more breaths ensued as she gulped down the fresh air. At this point she discovered that it tasted just like Earth air, which was such a blessing after being cooped-up in the confined space-egg for such a long period of time.

Once she was safely on the ground, Amanda climbed out of her ejector seat and looked all about her. It was strange to see a green sky. She had always wondered why the sky was blue and the grass was green. Why couldn't it be the other way around, she had often thought? And now it was! It was certainly different – but nicely so. What was even stranger though, was the quantity of other planets that could be seen poking through the heavy cloud of gases above Laktose. And they were so colourful too.

Sometimes, back home on Earth, Amanda could see the moon on a clear, sunny day, and here on Laktose it seemed to be no different, except that it was possible to see lots of planets because they were situated so close together in the Milky Way.

Amanda placed the ejector seat back into the space-egg, removed her backpack from the cockpit and put the glass canopy into position. Then she pulled out a disposable camera and took several snapshots of the landscape, sky and surrounding planets.

"That should keep Dad happy," muttered Amanda as she slipped the camera into her backpack.

"Well, here goes…"

She took a few steps forward and then halted abruptly. Which way should she go, she wondered? Again, she looked around her. The landscape appeared to be the same in all directions, being nothing more than a vast expanse of seemingly never-ending blue grass – except for a yellowish outcrop on the distant horizon which resembled a large chunk of cheese. Amanda repeatedly shrugged her shoulders in despair at first, before finally deciding to set off towards the cheesy outcrop because it may at least provide a place to shelter if she became tired.

Having walked for an hour or more, a strong, somewhat familiar odour began to reach Amanda's nostrils as it wafted through the air, although she was not quite able to put her finger on exactly what it reminded her of. The smell became stronger and stronger until Amanda arrived at the top of a cliff where she peered over the edge to espy a vast ocean of white. It was only at that moment that Amanda recognised the familiar odour.

"*It's milk!*" she exclaimed, and then: "Why am I surprised? After all, this is the Milky Way."

As it turned out, there was a coastal path visible alongside the Sea of Milk, so Amanda decided to take it. After following the path for quite some time she noticed some white objects far in the distance which seemed to glisten, making them stand out from the contrasting colour of the blue grass. When she got nearer to the objects she realised that they appeared to be houses of some sort – lots of them, all clustered together – therefore, it was possibly a town. Next, she wondered what sort of reception she would receive from the townsfolk and felt extremely nervous about meeting the inhabitants of the planet Laktose. However, now that she had come this far she was certainly not about to go back.

CHAPTER SIX

Reunited with the Famous Captain Skelly

The houses drew closer and closer as she walked and, by the time Amanda arrived at the outskirts of the town, she could tell that it was large enough to actually be classified as a city. It nestled in a narrow valley that tapered down to meet the north shore of the Sea of Milk, giving the city an appearance of length rather than width, although several dwellings had also been built upon the steep banks of the valley. The houses were all dome-shaped, like igloos, and of a uniform size, but there were also other buildings of varying heights. They seemed to become larger the further away from the shoreline they were, and some of them were enormous – several storeys high and equally as long.

One building in particular stood out from the others, which was built upon a tall, thin mound that lay in the midst of the city. It reminded Amanda of a fairytale castle with its numerous turrets capped with tiny pointed roofs, and it was distinctly different from other buildings in the city. The only characteristic common with all of the buildings was that they were each constructed of the same white material, which no longer seemed to glisten now that Amanda was amongst them. Perhaps, Amanda thought, this was because the sky had now become a darker shade of green, casting a shadow over the whole landscape. It was, in fact, nightfall. It never became fully dark on Laktose, just duller, but Amanda would not have known this… There was a lot that Amanda had yet to find out about Laktose.

The city streets were deserted, with not a single soul in sight, so Amanda ventured in. At the very moment she stepped through the city gates, a loud, ear-piercing whistle sounded. Amanda froze on the spot, covering both of her ears with her hands in an attempt to drown out the noise. This whistle was actually an alarm call that heralded the start of the day for the inhabitants of the city, because the people of Laktose were creatures of habit. They always arose at the same hour every morning; they also went to work at the same time, came home at the same time and went to bed at the same time too. It was what they had always done throughout their history and it was what they would always do.

Once the high-pitched whistling had ceased, Amanda lowered her arms down by her sides. Then, within the next few seconds the inhabitants of the dome-shaped dwellings began to emerge and fill the lonely streets. When they spotted the girl their eyes widened in disbelief and excited chatter broke out amongst them. Some of them retreated to their abodes, reappearing seconds later with their families whom they had brought out to view this wondrous sight.

Very soon, the streets were packed with a river of folk who surrounded Amanda in every direction. Amanda stood perfectly still, not knowing what to do or say. She was just as awestruck as them for she could not get over the fact that they were so tiny. Of course, she realised that Skelly was only two feet tall, but she had never really given this much thought in the past, and she had certainly not imagined meeting a whole race of people the same size as him. However, this was exactly what she was witnessing now – everyone was precisely the same height, and there were no exceptions. So, at around four feet and ten inches tall, Amanda must have seemed like a giant to these people.

"Hi!" greeted Amanda, at the same instance holding her hand aloft and waving.

This seemed to frighten the gathered crowd and they immediately dived for the cover of their homes, their white, jelly-like flesh wobbling profusely as they fled. Amanda giggled at this.

"You can come out now," she shouted when the streets became deserted again. "Don't be afraid… I don't bite," and she giggled some more.

Slowly, the city dwellers began to poke their heads out of their doorways and creep back onto the streets.

"BOO!" shouted Amanda as they grew nearer.

Once again, the tiny folk rapidly dispersed. How Amanda howled with laughter because she was enjoying playing this game with them.

"I'm only joking with you," she said with a chuckle. "I really am harmless."

But Amanda was having fun and when the little folk re-emerged she did it again.

"BOO!" she shrieked.

The crowd retreated but, this time, only for a short distance. At first they stayed back and muttered noisily amongst themselves. Then, without warning, they ran forward and surged all around her to sweep Amanda off her feet.

"Hey! I was just kidding," she yelled. "There's no need to be so rough with me."

Several burly members of the tiny crowd quickly pinned Amanda down, after which she was forcefully bundled into a torpedo-shaped, glass-covered capsule and hoisted into the air.

"Let me go," Amanda screamed at the top of her voice, "or I'll…" But Amanda did not really know what she would do.

After that, she was passed over the heads of the crowd in a gentle but rapid movement until the glass capsule arrived at an immensely tall building which towered high into the sky. There was no sign of a door in the building, but suddenly, as if by magic, one materialised out of nowhere, whereupon Amanda and the capsule were taken inside the building and inserted into a glass duct. During this snug fit a vacuum of air was created, which sent the capsule travelling in an upward direction. Up and up Amanda journeyed, passing swiftly through each level of the building until she arrived at the uppermost floor of the skyscraper. Whilst travelling, she had noticed that each floor of the cylindrical-shaped building was constructed from glass that had no visible means of support structures, and there were people on some floors – alone in isolated cells of glass that contained no doorways or windows. As far as Amanda could make out, this was a prison and she had been sent to the top level – furthest away from the ground – which, she imagined, possibly meant that she was now a maximum-security prisoner of the highest priority.

When the capsule came to a halt an aperture appeared in the glass pipe – again, as if by magic – which allowed Amanda to exit the torpedo-shaped capsule. However, as soon as she had stepped into the upper room, the aperture closed-up and the capsule travelled back down to ground level.

Amanda looked all around her and found that the room was virtually empty, except for an inflatable couch which appeared to hover, unaided, at a height of just several inches off the ground. After bumping her head, she quickly learned that she had to stoop down when she stood by the perimeter walls of the cell, forcing her to stand in the centre of the room in order to be more comfortable – although, even here, Amanda's head still brushed against the ceiling. It was obvious that the rooms had been built to a specific height which easily accommodated the race of people from Laktose, and they had never expected taller folk to visit their planet.

Completely encased in her glass cell, Amanda had an amazing view of the city and its surrounding landscape that included the Sea of Milk. If only she had her camera with her so that she could take some photographs for her father, she thought, but her backpack had been taken from her when she was bundled into the glass capsule. And, right now, Amanda so yearned to be at home with her mum and dad, for she felt very homesick – how she wished that she had not begun this trip!

After a brief examination of her new – somewhat stark – surroundings, Amanda discovered a small panel, together with a white button, situated on the wall of the dome. Although a little unsure, she pressed the button to see what would happen. The panel instantly slid aside and a large glass of milk appeared. Amanda was thirsty and she quickly gulped down the milk, which tasted extremely good. Following that, she began to feel sleepy because she had not slept for quite some time. The floating couch looked inviting, so Amanda took hold of it and lowered her body slowly down. When she lay on the couch her weight caused it to bob up and down until it found its own level and eventually settled down. It really was very comfortable and, feeling tired out from her epic journey, the young girl soon fell asleep.

Some time later Amanda awoke with a start, as if something had disturbed her. Feeling quite refreshed after her catnap, she stepped off the bed to discover that the glass capsule had returned for her. Its aperture was already open, beckoning her to step inside. So Amanda did just that, whereupon the capsule immediately whisked her back to ground level where half-a-dozen burly Laktosians awaited her arrival.

They carried the capsule in a strange contraption that Amanda could not even begin to describe, on a journey that took her through the streets of the city. She was lying on her back in the cramped capsule, therefore the only view she had was facing towards the sky. The streets were lined with people and Amanda could see the inquisitive expressions on their faces as she passed amongst them. She also noticed that the buildings were becoming smaller as she travelled, which led her to believe that they were taking her to the outskirts of the city for whatever reason.

Then she stopped moving altogether. There was an exchange of dialogue amongst her captors, which Amanda could not understand because their language was totally different to anything she had ever heard before and it was completely alien to her. A splashing sound then reached her ears, like waves lapping onto a shore. Amanda guessed that she was near to the Sea of Milk, and it turned out that she was. She and the capsule were placed into a vessel, similar to a pencil-shaped speedboat, and her companions climbed aboard also. The vessel sped across the Sea of Milk, gliding smoothly over the surface of the liquid without making a single ripple and neither was there any sound whatsoever from its twin engines. Amanda wondered where she was being taken to, and she was feeling extremely frightened by the whole experience.

Very soon the vessel entered a cove, at which point a door opened inwards upon a smooth rock-face. Once inside, Amanda and the capsule were inserted into a glass pipe – just like the one in the tall building she had left behind – and a vacuum of air forced the capsule upward. She emerged in a brightly-lit room where the capsule opened automatically, allowing her to step out of it. Feeling a little stiff after her cramped journey, Amanda stood erect and stretched her aching limbs. Then she watched as her six burly guards followed suit, each one having moulded their flexible bodies into a torpedo-shape so that they too could travel along the pipe.

One by one, the little men popped back into shape before frog-marching her to a podium in the centre of the room. Amanda climbed onto the raised platform and found that she could stand up with ease because of the high ceiling overhead.

Seating was arranged around the podium in a circular, terraced fashion and every single seat was taken up by spectators, who were regarding Amanda with keen interest. Amanda trembled like a leaf in a breeze, terrified of whatever fate awaited her.

One of the spectators sat upon a tall throne, which allowed the little fellow to have direct eye-contact with the girl. He looked very important and Amanda assumed him to be the leader because, when the audience were not watching her, all eyes were upon him. When he had finished scrutinising the Earth girl, the man raised both of his hands in the air; in response to which, one of the guards immediately walked up to the throne and handed him a bulky-looking object.

"Hey! That's my backpack," shouted Amanda.

There was a unanimous cry of "Ooh-ga" from the audience and they glared at Amanda in disgust.

Having detected what she guessed as being a note of annoyance in their cry, Amanda assumed that she was not supposed to speak out of turn, so she corrected herself.

"Sorry!" she apologised.

The important-looking man spread the contents of Amanda's backpack onto a table in front of him. Then there was another gasp of "Ooh-ga" from the crowd when they saw the strange array that was Amanda's belongings. Following that, there was a silence, as if they were waiting for something. As it turned out, they were! Just moments into this lapse of silence the congregation turned their gaze towards the entrance and then got to their feet amidst a huge round of applause as a late arrival popped out of the pipe.

Amanda could not see the new member's face because he – or she – was wearing a space helmet. She assumed that it was a he, though, because everyone else in the room was male, apart from her. And she also guessed that the visitor was an eminent person too, due to the fact that everyone bowed when the figure approached the important-looking man.

This eminent person wore a long cloak that dragged on the ground behind him and had bright red epaulettes upon each shoulder. He removed the helmet, standing with his back to Amanda as he spoke to the man who was seated upon the throne in their strange language. Then she saw him pick up one of the items from her backpack and browse at it briefly before reeling around.

"*AMANDA!*" the eminent person exclaimed at the top of his voice.

"*SKELLY?* Skelly… Is that really you?"

A burble of excited banter erupted throughout the room when the visitor dropped his space helmet and, still clutching Amanda's teddy bear in his hands, bounded onto the podium to throw his arms around the girl in pure delight.

"Oh, Skelly," cried Amanda, tears of joy streaming down her cheeks. "I'm so pleased to see you – I've been so scared."

"There's nothing here to be frightened of," Skelly assured her. "What a nice surprise this is, and so unexpected… What are you doing here? More to the point, how did you get here?"

"It's a long story," Amanda replied, but before she could say anything else the important man cleared his throat loudly in order to get their attention.

"Oh, please excuse me Amanda," said Skelly. "I have a lot of explaining to do to our king."

Having said this, using his mother tongue, Skelly launched into a deep conversation with his ruler. Whilst they talked Amanda noticed that the congregation were whispering amongst themselves and nodding their heads in approval, as if they were finally beginning to understand who she was. Eventually, the conversation ended and silence reigned once more as the king of Laktose stepped down from his throne, gesturing to Amanda to be seated in his place. Meanwhile, Amanda looked a little apprehensive.

"Come," said Skelly, reassuringly. "The king is offering you his seat, which is truly an honour and a privilege, never before seen on Laktose."

Skelly led Amanda to the throne, where she sat down. She had initially thought that the throne had seemed a little too large for the king but it fitted her perfectly. The ruler, King Sizemars, began to talk nineteen-to-the-dozen once she was seated, and Amanda could not understand a single word he said. However, Skelly quickly came to the rescue as he translated word for word.

"It is indeed an honour to welcome you to Laktose," said the king. "I apologise profusely for frightening you; it was not meant to be that way. You see, we thought you were a goddess from a distant galaxy and we weren't sure how to deal with you, so we brought you here to await the arrival of Captain Skelly. We knew that he would know what to do... I would like to bestow upon you the freedom of the planet of Laktose, to come and go as you please… and we hope that you enjoy your stay here."

Naturally, Amanda accepted the apology. Then the entire congregation filed up to Amanda, shook her hand and bowed to her. The king was last in the queue, and he bowed lower than anyone else. Afterwards, everyone exited through the pipe, leaving Amanda and Skelly alone.

"*Captain Skelly?*" said Amanda in an enquiring voice.

Skelly grinned.

"We have a lot of news to catch up on," he told her. "It will have to wait until tomorrow, though – it's been a long day for all of us."

The exhausted girl nodded her head in agreement because she felt so tired that she could hardly keep her eyes open.

"Come along then," said Skelly. "I have my own transport so you can travel with me."

Amanda hurriedly shoved her belongings back into her backpack and they too exited via the glass duct – which, Skelly explained, was called a Supa-Tube Elevator – before departing on Skelly's space-scooter. Once again, this was a silent form of transport that hovered above the ground.

Amanda sat behind her friend in a comfortable bucket seat as they zoomed over the Sea of Milk. She looked over her shoulder at the small island they had left behind but she could not see it because it had apparently become invisible. Amanda later learned that the secret island only appeared on special occasions, and only when requested by the king.

Following a short journey Skelly returned Amanda to the tall building where she had previously been held captive.

"If I have the freedom of the planet Laktose, then why have you brought me back to this prison?" Amanda asked in dismay.

Skelly laughed heartily at this.

"It's not a prison… It's a hotel!" he informed her with a chuckle. "And the higher up you are in the building, the more important you are."

"Then I must be very important," said Amanda, "because I've been put on the top floor."

"Yes, you are very important," replied Skelly.

Amanda smiled warmly.

"Goodnight Skelly – It's really nice to see you again."

"It's nice to see you too Amanda… Goodnight."

"Oh, one more thing before you go – How will I know when it's morning?" she asked. "It never seems to get dark here."

"You'll hear the alarm call," Skelly told her. "You can't miss it; it's a high-pitched whistling sound."

Amanda remembered it well.

"I'll come and collect you just after the alarm has sounded," added Skelly. "Goodnight."

With that, Skelly departed. Amanda was about to ask him how she could get to her room but he had already disappeared. There was no cause for concern though, because a capsule automatically arrived to pick her up. She climbed aboard and was transported to the upper floor, where she spent some time gazing out of the glass dome at the city all around her. The streets far below were deserted once again, therefore she guessed that it must be nightfall. So Amanda went to bed.

CHAPTER SEVEN

Amanda Learns to Speak Laktosian

As promised, Skelly arrived in the morning to collect Amanda, who was already waiting to greet him at the foot of the skyscraper hotel.

"I'm starving," she announced. "I've finished off the last packet of chocolate biscuits that I brought with me and I don't know where I will be able to get any more."

It then dawned on Skelly that nobody on Laktose would have been able to tell Amanda how to order food because they could not speak her language. Therefore, he was the only person on the planet who could converse with her and he had been away on his travels when she had first arrived there.

"Oh, you poor thing," Skelly said sympathetically. "There's a panel on the wall in your hotel room with a white button beside it: press it once for milk and twice to get food from room service."

"I've already found out how to get milk," Amanda told him, "but how do I ask for food when I can't speak your language?"

"You don't have to ask. There are pictures on the menu; just touch the one you would like to eat and your choice of food will instantly appear."

"What a great idea," said Amanda. "I'll have to go and try it out."

"Not right now," said Skelly. "Hop onto the back of my scooter and I'll take you to my favourite café for breakfast – It's a milk bar several blocks from here."

Together, they cruised through the streets and thoroughfares that were already teeming with people. Amanda was still something of a novelty in their midst and many people stopped to stare at her. This made Skelly feel very important as he piloted his celebrity companion through the city.

The milk bar was virtually empty when they arrived, but word quickly spread that a guest from another world – together with a famous Space Captain – were dining at the café and, very soon, it was heaving with sight-seers anxious to catch a glimpse of the two celebrities. However, the attention they were receiving became so unbearable that the pair had to make a quick exit through the back door before they had even had a chance to order breakfast. Skelly then took Amanda to a fly-thru diner instead, which was just like a drive-thru back on Earth, where they ordered breakfast to take back to Amanda's hotel so that they could eat in peace and quiet.

"So much for dining out," remarked Skelly.

"Quite!" Amanda replied, wiping the last few crumbs from the corner of her mouth. "Never mind – it would have been just as delicious no matter where we had eaten."

She had just eaten burger and fries, which tasted much better than it looked. Skelly had advised her that some things were a little mixed up on Laktose so he had ordered breakfast on her behalf. For instance: burger and fries on the menu would actually have been broccoli and sprouts; so he had, in fact, ordered broccoli and sprouts, which was really burger and fries! And, not only were these dishes the wrong way around, but their appearance was also the opposite.

Skelly explained that Laktose was slightly topsy-turvy because there were so many other planets in the Milky Way which affected its gravitational pull. This was the very reason why Amanda had arrived in her space-egg flying upside down when, in reality, she wasn't. And it was also the reason for the grass being blue and the sky being green. It was a little confusing but that was how it was and she would soon get used to it.

When they had finished eating their meal, the duo sat together and exchanged stories. Amanda told Skelly all that had happened since his departure from Earth, and Skelly related his tale too...

When Skelly had arrived back at the planet Laktose he was instantly hailed as a hero. It had been so many years since his disappearance that his mother and father had given him up for good. Obviously, they were delighted to be re-united with their long-lost son and a huge party was announced for his home-coming. Skelly was guest of honour at the party, of course, which was to be held at the grand palace of King Sizemars, high on the mound at the far end of the city. All of the city dwellers were invited and not a single person failed to attend.

Because of his outstanding contribution to space travel and his extensive knowledge of distant planets, Skelly was knighted 'Captain Skelly' at a special ceremony organised by the king himself. Skelly was over the moon (and several other planets too!) for this meant that he also had a new job. In effect, he was now a space explorer who spent much time away from home travelling around the universe. To give his job title in full, he was actually an Inter-Planetary Ambassador and Interpreter of Universal Languages.

Visiting the billions of planets in the Milky Way was a full-time occupation in itself, but Skelly also had to incorporate long-distance trips in order for him to receive his monthly bonus, which was paid in the form of extra days off work. The job was very tiring because it entailed extensive time travel, sometimes leaping many light years in just one move, and this tiredness was known as rocket-lag, which was caused by travelling through different time zones. Thankfully, his body had soon adjusted to suit his new lifestyle and he loved the job with a passion.

Skelly told Amanda that he would be embarking on a return mission to Earth at some time in the future, although he could not say for sure exactly when that would be.

"I have a date pencilled-in on my lunar calendar," he said, "but I really don't know where I'm going from one month to the next."

"Your destiny is in the stars," laughed Amanda.

"Yes, it's just a phase I'm going through," joked Skelly. "You're not laughing… Phase – get it? Phase of the moon!"

"Yes, of course I get it – it's just not very funny," groaned Amanda.

"I Apollo-gise," Skelly continued.

Amanda failed to understand that joke as well because she was far too young. So Skelly had to explain that the Apollo moon missions were launched from Earth in the late 1960s and early 1970s. Amanda had lost interest by then and she changed the subject slightly.

"Why do you wear a space helmet?" she asked. "You didn't wear one when you left Earth and I never had to wear one to travel here."

"Oh, it's purely for show," Skelly replied. "Mind you, I do need to wear it sometimes when I'm in deep space, especially if I'm travelling through black holes, for instance, when it tends to get quite bumpy."

"Do you know anything about black holes Skelly?"

"Yes… quite a lot actually," he replied, "but I don't mean to sound bigheaded."

Amanda didn't think that Skelly was a bighead at all.

"Maybe you could talk to my dad about them," she said. "He'd love to hear any information about black holes that he can get."

"I'd be glad to help him. I'll see what I can do on my next visit to Earth," Skelly agreed.

"Oh, I'm so happy to see you again Skelly," said Amanda, suddenly throwing her arms around him and giving him a big hug.

"And it's great to see you too Amanda – I've missed you terribly. I shall never forget the adventures that we had together."

"Me neither," said Amanda in a voice tinged with sadness. "It's such a pity that those moments couldn't last forever."

"I'm sure we shall have further adventures," said Skelly. "Surely this is an adventure for you right now."

"Yes, I guess it is," Amanda agreed.

"And, as luck would have it, I'm home on leave for the summer holidays," said Skelly. "I've got a whole month off work, so I'll be able to show you some of the sights of Laktose and that will be an adventure in itself."

"I can't wait... Where do we begin?"

"Well, for a start, I'd like you to meet my parents."

"That'll be cool," said Amanda. "When?"

"There's no time like the present," said Skelly, and then there was a slight pause before he added: "...the past, and the future."

Amanda stared at him blankly.

"That's just one of my sayings," he told her, but Amanda was still none the wiser. "Anyway, my parents live quite a way from here, so you'll need to bring an overnight bag with you."

"I've only got my backpack and that's already packed," Amanda eagerly said.

"Well, what are we waiting for? Come on... let's go."

They jumped onto Skelly's space-scooter and set out towards the edge of the city (which, Amanda learned, was called Kallseum), climbing high into the air so that the tall structures could be avoided. Skelly skilfully circled around the fairytale palace, proudly pointing out its magnificent features to Amanda. Then they descended to a more stable height, several inches from the ground, as they resumed the journey across open terrain.

Whilst en-route the pair stopped and watched the planets go down over the Purple Lakes of Peace. Skelly explained that the lakes got their shading from the reflection of the blue grass and the deep crimson rock of the lake bed which, when combined together, made the colour purple.

The evening air was still and warm, as it always was on Laktose, for there was no such thing as wind. This was due, in part, to the close proximity of the neighbouring planets that blocked out any turbulence, and also because the gravity was equally balanced on the surface.

It was almost nightfall when the pair arrived at Skelly's parents' home. Skelly told Amanda that this was where they had moved to when his mistaken voyage to Earth had occurred all those years ago, and this is where they had lived ever since. They had wanted to escape the hustle and bustle of the city – just like Amanda's mum and dad had done – and they considered themselves very fortunate indeed to be able to live in the open landscape because not many people on Laktose were given that opportunity. Amanda could understand why they had moved here: it was a truly beautiful setting with the Purple Lakes just a stone's throw away, the Cheddar Mountains looming high on the horizon and the marvellous planet rises and sets that could be seen from this part of Laktose.

Amanda noticed that the house was large by Laktosian standards – certainly in comparison to the size of the dwellings she had seen in the city at least. Perhaps, she thought, this was because they were so tightly packed together in the city there was little choice but to build smaller houses. As yet, she had not seen the interior of a Laktosian house so she was quite excited at this prospect and even more excited that she was going to meet Skelly's parents. Skelly had told them he was going to be visiting but he had not warned them he was bringing a friend with him.

As usual, there was no visible door through which to enter the building, but Skelly placed his hand upon the outer wall and a doorway magically appeared. His parents then rushed to greet him, whereupon you could only imagine their surprise when they set eyes upon Amanda. They jabbered away like over-excited monkeys at first, pulling all sorts of strange faces as they talked to Skelly, then they held out their hands towards Amanda in a welcoming gesture.

Amanda shook their hands and smiled nervously, staring at her hosts in wonderment. She found it difficult to get over their incredible likeness to Skelly. It was quite uncanny, for they were almost a carbon copy of their son. They had the same cute little button noses, large saucer-shaped eyes, elfin-like ears, and fine tufts of transparent fur that rested on top of their heads, although their body shapes were a lot rounder than Skelly's.

"Hello," said Skelly's father and mother at the same time.

Amanda was almost struck dumb.

"*You speak my language!*" she gasped.

But they didn't answer her. Instead, they reverted to Laktosian-speak – a language that sounded like pure gibberish to Amanda.

"They didn't understand you," Skelly explained. "I have been trying to teach them Earth language but it takes time to learn… it's their generation, you know. So far, 'hello' is the only word they have managed to learn. However, a friend of mine has recently produced an aid that will enable people to convert languages, so that whatever language is being used will be heard and spoken fluently."

"It would be so cool to be able to speak Laktosian. How does this aid work?" asked Amanda.

"It's a device that attaches under the chin which automatically converts your speech to match the dialogue you are hearing."

"What a clever idea… I wonder why nobody has thought of it before. It would be so useful back home as well because there are so many different languages spoken throughout our world."

"It's exactly the same here in deep space," said Skelly, "although many galaxies, such as the Milky Way, talk in a universal tongue. All the same though, my friend's speech-converter will not become mass-produced because I will be out of a job."

Amanda looked at him quizzically.

"How so?" she asked.

"It's too revolutionary. I'm supposed to be an Inter-Galactic Interpreter; therefore, if everyone has a speech-converter, multi-lingual speakers would become ten-a-penny and there will no longer be a need for me."

"I see," said Amanda, nodding her head understandingly. "But what will you do with any speech-converters that have already been made?"

"I shall keep them for myself because they will make my job easier as well as make me seem clever in the eyes of other people. I'll need some spares anyway, just in case of breakages. While you are here you may as well make use of one as well."

"Thanks," Amanda said gleefully. "I promise I'll take great care of it…"

Skelly's parents were still chattering noisily between themselves and he could no longer hear what Amanda was saying, so he began to sing at the top of his voice. Amanda joined in too, because she also knew the song.

The words they sang came from a 1950s rock and roll number that was in Amanda's father's old record collection, which Skelly had become quite fond of listening to during his stay at their house. In fact, when he had blasted off to return to his home planet, he had listened to it all the way home – over and over again – because Amanda's dad had made a recording especially for him to play through his space-egg's quadraphonic sound system.

Skelly's parents put their fingers into their ears, staring at Amanda and Skelly in horror as they sang their song. It had the desired effect though, for they immediately went quiet. Then Skelly interpreted the conversation as his parents apologised to Amanda for talking over the top of them and being so rude. But it was hard work for Amanda to make conversation with such a vast language barrier and there were long silences. During one of these silences Skelly mysteriously disappeared, albeit only for a brief time because he returned shortly afterwards with something in his hand.

"Try this," said Skelly as he handed the object to Amanda.

"What is it?" she asked.

"It's a speech converter."

Amanda stared at the object warily.

"It looks more like a sticking-plaster," she said, "something similar to a Band-Aid!"

"That's exactly what it is – a sticking-plaster in disguise – but it is impregnated with a miniscule computer system, hidden in the padded part, which transmits and receives voice waves."

Feeling rather foolish, Amanda stuck the plaster beneath her chin as directed by Skelly, while he watched her do this.

"Well... say something," he said rather impatiently. "I'm dying to see whether it works."

"What do you want me to say?" asked Amanda, but it came out as gobbledigook – yet, at the same time, she understood what she had said.

"Gosh! I can speak Laktosian," Amanda whooped excitedly.

"*Shiddleydootz!* It works... It works..." cried Skelly, leaping up and down in delight.

Not being able to converse with Amanda when Skelly had suddenly vanished, his parents had gone off to prepare a bedroom for their unexpected Earth guest; so, having heard the commotion, they rushed back into the room.

"What's all the fuss about son?" asked Skelly's father, with a look of concern on his rotund face.

"I was just trying out this new device that Skelly's friend has invented," Amanda told them.

With their mouths wide open they gawped at the girl in astonishment, finding it hard to believe that she had mastered the Laktosian language in such a short period of time. Finally, Skelly's father spoke up.

"Is that a Band-Aid under your chin?" he asked Amanda.

"Yes," she replied.

"Have you hurt yourself, then?"

"No, I haven't," Amanda said, feeling quite awkward about wearing the sticking-plaster. "I'll let Skelly explain."

Even though Skelly spent the rest of the evening trying to explain what the device did, his parents found it hard to grasp, preferring to believe that Amanda was a super-intelligent Earth child who could learn things really quickly. In the end Skelly gave up and everyone went to bed, for it was now that time of night when all of the planet's inhabitants fell asleep.

Amanda had been given a generously-proportioned room which had the highest ceiling in the house. Once again, the bed was a floating one, just like the couch in her hotel room – it appeared that this tended to be the trend on the planet. Amanda climbed aboard and immediately fell asleep, thoroughly exhausted after her day's experiences. No sooner had she fallen asleep though, when she was rudely awakened. She froze in terror as the bottom of her bed began to dip towards the floor and then started to bounce up and down. Then she felt the weight of something on top of her that was slowly working its way along her body, gently patting her as it moved closer to her head. She raised her head off the pillow so that she could see what was attacking her, but there was nothing to be seen. This was the final straw. Amanda could take no more and she began to scream the house down.

Skelly appeared in a trice, an anxious look written all over his face. His parents were quickly in tow.

"What's the matter, Amanda?" he asked.

"Something was attacking me," she cried. "I think it's still on my bed, but I'm not sure because I can't see it!"

Skelly leant forward to touch the bed, and then he burst out laughing. He said something to his mum and dad and they too laughed heartily. Amanda could not understand what was being said because she did not have the speech-converter in place.

"Wh... wh... what?" she stammered. "What's so funny?"

"There's nothing to worry about," Skelly assured her when he eventually managed to stop laughing. "It's only Creampuff – he's our pet Laktopuss."

"But I can't see him," said Amanda. "Where is he?"

"He's on your pillow. You won't be able to see him because he's invisible. The only time a Laktopuss can be seen is when they get wet. I'm so sorry he frightened you Amanda – it never crossed my mind to warn you about him... But it really is funny."

"Yeah, hilarious," Amanda said, rather sarcastically. "So, what does Creampuff look like?"

"Well, he's about eighteen inches in length, has four long floppy ears, eight legs – four with paws and four with flippers (because he likes to swim a lot) that double as wings – and he's got long white fur too. He doesn't fly much though, because he's still in his development stages… That's about it really."

"Golly! How could there possibly be anything else? I mean, he's got a bit of several species of animal in him by the sound of it. And what do you mean that he's in the development stages still?"

"Laktopussi originally existed on only one particular planet of the Milky Way. They are no longer there now because they were hunted to extinction. The Ancient Laktosians – a lost race known as the Whispering Shylots – brought the last surviving pair to our planet many moons ago and we have bred them from that pair. Every household on Laktose has one now – it's the only species of animal that exists here."

"I know that we can't see him but I was wondering… is it possible to feel him?" asked Amanda.

"Of course – go ahead and touch him. When he's hungry you'll be able to hear him too because he barks like a cat!"

Amanda gave Skelly a questioning look as she felt around on her bed for the creature.

"It makes a sound like a mixture of a yap and a meow," explained Skelly.

"Kind of like a yeow, then," joked Amanda.

By this time she had located the whereabouts of the Laktopuss.

"Ooh, he feels so soft," she exclaimed. "It's just like touching velvet."

"Hmmm," murmured Skelly in agreement, holding his hand over his mouth as he yawned. "Do you mind if I go to bed now? I'll take Creampuff with me so that he doesn't annoy you any more."

"No! I mean… yes, go to bed, but you can leave Creampuff with me, if you don't mind."

"Okay," Skelly replied with a grin on his face. "I'll leave him in your room… he'll keep you warm and he'll be a comfort to you also."

With that, he left the room. Then Amanda climbed back onto her bed, where Creampuff instantly settled down beside her pillow, just as her cat Tabs always did every night. It was quite comforting to have the Laktopuss by her side, purring gently into her ear, because it reminded her of being in her own bed at home on Earth. Oh, how she already missed her home – and her parents, and Tabs, and Milkstar too – because she was feeling quite homesick again at that present moment in time. A tear rolled down her cheek as she thought about everyone and everything back on Earth. All the same, very soon she fell asleep.

CHAPTER EIGHT

Amanda and Skelly Go Planet Surfing

Amanda was just about to nod off to sleep in a comfortable floating chair when Skelly walked into the room and disturbed her.

"Are you ready to go now?" he asked.

The girl stood up and stretched her tired limbs.

"Yes, I'm ready," Amanda replied, once she had finished yawning. "I don't know why I feel so tired; we've hardly done anything today."

"It's probably the planet's atmosphere – It takes a bit of getting used to," suggested Skelly. "Anyway, if you're ready, let's go and have some fun."

They had spent a lazy morning along the shores of the Purple Lakes, drifting around in a large, round boat with high sides – shaped rather like a breakfast bowl, Amanda thought. Skelly had told her that the boat was called a milk float because that was basically what it did, owing to the fact that there was no wind or waves to move it around. He also said that this was the true meaning of the term milk float, as opposed to the version found on Earth which milkmen drove around in. Regardless of all that, it was indeed an extremely peaceful and relaxing way to spend the morning, just lolling around with not a care in the world.

Creampuff had gone along with them for his daily exercise that consisted of a walk, a swim and then a fly, in that order. Once he had been immersed in the milky lake he became instantly visible, giving Amanda a chance to see what he really looked like. She found the animal to be highly comical when he walked because his eight limbs moved alternatively, in pairs, so that there were always four in the air at any one time, giving him the impression of a mobile windmill.

He came into his own when he swam though, gliding gracefully across the lake's surface as his broad flippers splayed outwards to silently propel him along. Every now and again Creampuff would dive into the milky depths of the lake and then break the surface at speed, launching his body high into the air. Then he inverted his flippers to form wings which flapped manically as he attempted to stay airborne. But poor Creampuff could only manage a short distance before he plummeted into the lake like a lead weight. Skelly explained to Amanda that the clumsy creature was still a beginner at the flying lark, therefore it may well take some time to perfect his art, although he was confident that it would eventually happen. Having watched the ungainly animal's pathetic attempts at flight, Amanda had her doubts and fully believed that Skelly was purely trying to convince himself of this.

Exhausted by his efforts, the Laktopuss then took time out to recover by floating upon his back, his whiskery, seal-like facial features raised above the lake's surface, gulping down huge mouthfuls of air as he tried to regain his composure.

Whilst they watched Creampuff's humorous antics Skelly promised Amanda that he would take her planet surfing later that day, and that was exactly what they did.

When they arrived at the Cheddar Mountains Skelly parked his hover-scooter in the scooter bays and collected his ticket from the parking attendant, with the arrangement that he would collect it in a day or two. Next, they took the Supa-Tube Elevator to the highest mountain peak. The view from here was truly spectacular. Amanda could see virtually half of the planet from this point, including the Purple Lakes, and she could make out the city of Kallseum on the distant horizon, with its numerous buildings rising up to become silhouetted beside the vast Sea of Milk. She quickly whipped out the camera from the top pocket of her jacket and took some stunning photographs for her father – she was sure that he was going to be extremely proud of her for taking such fantastic pictures.

Then she turned around to look at what she had really come to see. Several bands of liquid rose from either side of the mountain peak, disappearing high into the outer atmosphere of the planet before cascading downwards in an arc until they met the next range of mountains. These impressive bands of liquid were apparently called wheybridges because they were made from whey (a watery residue obtained from milk and used for making cheese) and linked each mountain range just like a bridge span. It was therefore possible to surf around the entire planet using these wheybridges, eventually ending up at the starting point on top of the Cheddar Mountains, which was the source of all wheybridges.

Amanda was really excited at the prospect of surfing around Laktose but when she saw the long queue of people who were waiting their turns her face fell in dismay. She had been so taken-in by the marvellous sights that she had not noticed the crowd until now; however, they had noticed her! From the moment she and Skelly had popped out of their Supa-Tube capsules all eyes had been upon them; and her in particular. Everyone on Laktose had heard about the girl's presence on their planet by now and they knew that she was hanging out with the famous Captain Skelly, so they could not believe what they were seeing when the famous duo arrived at the top of the Cheddar Mountains together.

"I wasn't expecting it to be quite so busy," said Skelly in a disappointed voice. "I had completely forgotten that it was the summer holidays and the kids would all be off school."

"Never mind," Amanda consoled him. "It's much the same as it is on Earth... everyone heads for the holiday attractions and there's always a mile-long queue. We'll just have to be patient and wait our turns."

But they did not have to wait for very long because the youngsters moved aside to let the celebrities go to the front of the line.

"Oh, no!" said Amanda, turning down their offers of chivalry. "We're nobody special; we really couldn't..."

"Thank you good people, we're much obliged," Skelly interrupted by shouting loudly in order to drown out Amanda's thoughtful speech. Then he grabbed her by the arm and led her forwards.

"Never look a gift horse in the mouth," he muttered quietly. "We'll be here all day if we wait for the queue to go down... You go first."

Amanda stepped into the shiny glass surfball. It was a bit of a squeeze though, because they were built to take the tiny figures of the Laktosian race. Nevertheless, she managed to fit inside quite comfortably. She placed her feet into the two fibreglass stirrups that would support her, and then she grabbed hold of the aluminium steering rod that ran in a horizontal direction across the ball in front of her.

"What do I have to do?" asked Amanda.

"Just hold on tight to that rod, and steer by using the weight of your body to alter course – the surfball will go in the direction you move and the wheybridge will do all of the work for you... Don't worry, I won't be far behind you," yelled Skelly.

Then the invisible door sealed itself shut and Amanda was launched on the ride of her lifetime. At first, she was all over the place – upside down, sideways, backwards and spinning around and around – but she soon got the hang of it. The rivers of whey flowed smoothly in a constant direction to begin with, until they reached the highest point of the wheybridge. It was only then that Amanda began to experience the true exhilaration of planet surfing. She quickly learned that the glass surfball accelerated as the liquid began to pour downwards – just like a roller-coaster – forcing Amanda to hang on for dear life. She fought every inch of the way, using all of her might as she heroically managed to control the runaway surfball, which was going faster and faster with every passing second, while the next range of mountains were getting closer and closer.

It was at this point when Amanda suddenly realised that nobody had told her how to stop the surfball and she started to panic. But her anxiety was short-lived because a net suddenly appeared out of nowhere, slowing down her progress before whisking her safely from the liquid whey. Amanda's heart was pounding like a drum when the giant fishing net lowered her slowly onto the mountaintop. Following this, the crowd of people who had assembled at the whey station cheered loudly as the girl emerged from the surfball. She had to be helped to a chair, mind you, because her legs had gone all wobbly and she felt quite giddy too. Oh, but how she had enjoyed it: in fact, she could hardly wait for the next leg of the journey. Skelly arrived shortly afterwards, by which time Amanda had fully recovered from her experience and was eager to continue.

"What do you think of the ride?" panted Skelly as he was helped to a waiting chair for his recovery period.

"It's great fun!" Amanda replied. "See you later, Skelly." And off she went before her little friend could say anything else, because she was having way too much fun to find time to stop and chat.

There were a dozen wheybridges in total, some of which were longer than others, and it was impossible to complete the course in just one day, so Amanda and Skelly stayed overnight in the Mountain Lodge Surf Resort where they made lots of new friends amongst the guests. It was the middle of the following day when they eventually ended up at the point from where they had originally set out. Amanda vowed that she would have to do the whole planet surf course at least one more time before her return to Earth, and Skelly promised that he would bring her back. Having said goodbye to their new friends, the duo then returned to Skelly's parents' home.

Upon their arrival, Creampuff greeted them enthusiastically. Although he was invisible, his two tails could be felt whipping furiously against their legs as the creature darted between them.

They had arrived just in time for dinner, to find that Skelly's mum – in an attempt to make Amanda feel more at home – had prepared a lovely meal of fish and chips, using a recipe that she had found on the Intergalactic Internet. It was a most welcome change from some of the bland-tasting food that Amanda had so far consumed during her stay on the planet and it tasted just like the real thing.

"Your mum's a great cook," Amanda said to Skelly later that evening, just before they went to bed.

"Yes, she tries hard," Skelly agreed. "Mum loves to entertain guests and she's always willing to try out new recipes."

Amanda was deep in thought for a few moments before speaking again.

"I still don't know what your parents' names are, though," she said.

"I'm sorry; I never gave it a thought to tell you... Actually, they are both called Skelly, just like me."

"Oh, yes! Now I remember you telling me, not long after I met you, that everyone on Laktose is called Skelly... I think I'm going to find it rather confusing."

"Perhaps you should call them Mr. and Mrs. Jelly," suggested Skelly.

"*Mr. and Mrs. Jelly?*" Amanda scoffed. "That's your last name – *Jelly!*"

"Yes," replied Skelly, suddenly becoming defensive. "What's wrong with that? It's a common name here, just as Smith is a common name where you come from."

"Well, it sounds so funny. Fancy naming you Skelly Jelly!"

"It's not my fault," said Skelly, scornfully. "I was too young to say anything at my christening. Anyway, we don't really use surnames on Laktose except to address our elders as a mark of respect."

"SKELLY JELLY," Amanda mockingly chanted, and then she began to giggle.

"It's not a laughing matter," snapped Skelly. "I don't make fun of your name – Amanda James... Huh! James is a boy's name, anyway."

"No, it's not!" Amanda retorted. She had stopped giggling by now.

"Yes, it is... I remember a boy at your school called James Smith."

"So what? Besides, everybody called him Jim anyway."

"See! You don't like it when the ball's on the other foot, do you?" laughed Skelly.

"Okay, I give up... Let's call it a truce," Amanda surrendered.

She had found the whole ordeal to be rather a strange feeling – having an argument with Skelly, that is – and it was something that rarely occurred. Amanda did not even know how it had really began, but that is exactly how arguments start and then get out of hand before you know it.

Skelly willingly accepted the truce and the matter was quickly forgotten once they had made up. After that, the friends bid each other goodnight before retiring to their bedrooms. As soon as she had made herself comfortable, Amanda felt her floating bed sag when Creampuff climbed onto it again. Then he went through his usual rigmarole of paddling his way over her body before eventually settling down beside her head. However, she was used to him doing this by now and it didn't bother her in the slightest.

CHAPTER NINE

Kidnapped by the Rottanegs

One of the things that Amanda really liked about Laktose was the fact that everything was free. In other words, quite literally, you simply didn't have to pay for anything. It was not necessary for people to earn a wage because there was no such thing as money in the Milky Way; therefore, the only reason that the planet's inhabitants went to work every day was purely for something to do. So, instead of money there was a bartering system in force, whereupon people swapped something they no longer wanted for something they did need.

Every lunar month there was a space bazaar – also known as the black market – which was held on the planet Rhom, just a short journey away from Laktose. It so happened that during Amanda's visit there was going to be a bazaar day and Skelly was taking her to experience the event. He had told her that any object she had from Earth would be worth a small fortune – such as one of her disposable cameras, her watch, or her torch – therefore, she could eventually be returning to Earth with some very valuable items in her possession.

In order to get to Rhom it was necessary to catch the space bus that went via the planet Nim, where they had to hop onto a connecting bus that would take them to the bazaar at Rhom. So they caught the Nim bus and then the Rhom bus, arriving at the bazaar at around mid-morning. When they got there the bazaar was already bustling with people, bumping and jostling around in the hope of picking up a bargain or two. Amanda soaked up the atmosphere, enjoying every minute of it, for it reminded her of being at a busy London market, although with an altogether different range of goods on offer. In fact, she could not even hazard a guess as to what some of the objects on display were for, and neither did she even dare to ask.

There was a mixture of races in attendance from all over the Milky Way who had come to visit the bazaar at Rhom, but, as usual, Amanda was the centre of attention because people had never seen an alien that looked like her before. Amanda had braided her long hair into a French plait because she had become used to people on Laktose tugging and pulling at it, to the extent that it sometimes hurt her, and yet all sorts of people at the bazaar ran up to her and still did the same thing! She realised that it was a novelty to them and they meant no harm but, nevertheless, it was beginning to become rather annoying. Skelly soon came to her rescue though, because he found a large, lightweight vase on one of the stalls and he gave it to Amanda to wear as a protective hat. The vase had a handle, shaped like a teapot spout, sticking out of each side and she did look funny, although it seemed to do the trick because it stopped most of the harassment she was receiving.

Feeling rather stupid, but much happier at the prospect of being left alone, and following hot on the heels of Skelly,

Amanda forced her way through the crowded streets until something suddenly caught the girl's attention.

"Let's go and have a look at the stall over there, Skelly," said Amanda in an excited tone of voice.

But Skelly had seen an item on a nearby stall that was of greater interest to him and he was already deep in conversation with the stall-holder.

"You go ahead – I'll be over in just a moment or two," Skelly replied without even glancing upwards.

So Amanda approached the stall, peering between the passers-by as she tried to get a good look at the object that had caught her attention. Sure enough, when she managed to get through the crowd, Amanda was delighted to discover that the object was exactly what she thought it was – for it was none other than the miniature space egg... the very same one in which Boggles the lab rat had voyaged into orbit!

There were three sinister-looking beings behind the stall: a tall, hunched, skinny one; a really short, plump one; and another tall but really fat one. They all had dull, battleship grey skin that appeared to be as thick as elephant hide, with spiky black hair on top of their heads, and pointed, wedge-shaped faces that made them look like really ugly hedgehogs! They frothed hideously at their mouths and a foul-smelling odour lingered in the air about their persons too.

What Amanda did not realise was that these creatures were a notorious breed of scoundrel known as Rottanegs and it was not wise to speak to them in an offhand manner. The Rottanegs were not very nice people at all – in fact, that is a bit of an understatement because they are downright nasty individuals –

and this particularly wicked band of cut-throat thugs were actually time bandits who roamed throughout the galaxies, occasionally cropping up in the Milky Way. There was always a purpose for their presence too: usually because something of value was there for the taking, something that could be stolen in order to sell in a different time or galaxy. And you could always tell when the Rottanegs had paid you a visit because they left an awful eggy pong behind them, which is how they came by their dreadful name.

"Where did you get that?" Amanda said demandingly, pointing towards the space egg with one hand and pinching her nostrils with the other.

Whilst digesting Amanda's question, the three Rottanegs looked at each other in bewilderment, grunting ominously amongst themselves. Then, using the back of his hand, the skinny Rottaneg – who was called Blisterfoot – wiped away the froth from around his mouth and growled his reply.

"Mind your own business, Earth child!"

Upon hearing this retort the other two creatures burst into fits of laughter, while Blisterfoot joined in also, all three spraying spit and froth all over the place as they did so.

"Ooh, how gross!" muttered Amanda, gazing at the three stall-holders in disgust.

All of a sudden though, they stopped laughing, as if a switch had been turned off, and then it was the big creature's turn to grumble. His name was Blubberguts.

"Why do you ask?" he coughed at her.

"Because it belongs to me… well, to my dad actually, triangle-head!"

"Well, it belongs to us now," sneered Blisterfoot trying to imitate Amanda's voice, whilst totally oblivious of the fact she had just called him a name.

"I initially asked you a civil question and I expected a civil answer," she said angrily. "All I want to know is where you got that object."

"Oooohhh, get you," the three Rottanegs said together. *"Temper, temper!"*

Amanda felt a little intimidated by the three stall-holders but she stood her ground all the same. Pouting her lips and placing her hands on her hips, she impatiently tapped her foot on the ground.

"I'm not going away until you tell me where you got it," she snapped.

"We found it, if you must know," growled Blubberguts, finally giving in. "Finders-keepers; so there!"

Amanda opened her mouth to say something but nothing came out. She knew that they were not going to tell her exactly where they had found the space-egg; therefore it would be fruitless to continue the conversation. With a feeling of total despair she glanced in the direction of the small, plump Rottaneg who had not said a single word yet: all he had done so far was to stare at her, open-mouthed. Height-wise, this creature was more Amanda's size, so she felt capable of standing up to him.

"What's your problem?" she snapped at him. "Why do you keep staring at me?"

"Have you hurt your chin?" he asked. "It looks like you're wearing a Band-Aid."

"Oh, for goodness sake!" Amanda said with a sigh, for she was getting rather fed-up with people asking about it.

All three Rottanegs were now gawping at Amanda whilst they awaited the reply to their comrade's question, so she quickly tried to think of a reason for wearing it because she did not want to disclose the true identity of the sticking-plaster. In no time at all, she came up with the ideal excuse.

"I've got a pimple, okay? It's like a spot…"

"We know what a pimple is," roared the three Rottanegs in harmony, showering her heavily with froth.

"Yes, I'm sure you do," Amanda muttered as she wiped the saliva from her face. "Look, I'm obviously wasting my time here… I'm going to fetch my friend – he'll know how to deal with you over the space-egg. I'll be back in just a moment."

"No… Wait!" said Blubberguts in a much more gentle tone. "If you want to know where we obtained the space-egg, and if you really want it back, I can do a personal deal with you."

For a brief moment Amanda wondered why the creature had suddenly had such a change of heart. However, she did not look too deeply into the reason.

"Okay, tell me what the deal is," she said.

"I can't tell you in front of all these people," he said gesturing his hand towards the passers-by. "Why don't you step into my office and we'll discuss the matter in there?"

The big Rottaneg held aside the curtain which separated the front of the stall from the rear half and he beckoned Amanda to enter. All Amanda was interested in was finding out about the space-egg, so, unwittingly, she did what he requested. But, as soon as she had stepped inside the rear half of the stall,

Blubberguts grabbed hold of the girl and, placing one hand over her mouth to stifle her screams, he bundled her into a soundproof box and locked the lid tightly shut.

By this time Skelly had finished bartering with his stall-holder, albeit to no avail. So, having come away empty-handed, he then began to look all around him as he tried to locate the whereabouts of his absent friend. When he realised there was no sign of Amanda he set off along the line of market stalls, carefully searching amongst the crowd in the hope of catching a glimpse of her. Eventually, he arrived at the stall belonging to the Rottanegs, who were busily clearing away their goods.

"Have you seen a young girl – a human-type girl?" Skelly politely enquired.

"No!" Blisterfoot said, flatly.

"What does she look like?" asked the short, plump one, who went by the name of Bumblebutt.

Blisterfoot nudged his associate roughly.

"Shut-up, you fool!" he muttered, glowering at him.

"Well, she's quite a few inches taller than me, very pretty, and wearing a vase on her head," Skelly told the short Rottaneg, ignoring his associate's attempt at interfering in their conversation.

"Does she have a sticking-plaster on her chin?" continued Bumblebutt, who was a bit dim and was only trying to be helpful.

"Yes," replied Skelly. "Then, you must have seen her!"

At that moment the big Rottaneg hurriedly materialised from behind the curtain at the rear of the stall, grabbed the little one by the scruff of the neck and hurled him to one side.

"What he means is that she passed this way a short while ago," growled Blubberguts. "She only stayed very briefly and then disappeared in that direction," he lied, pointing a grisly, gnarled digit towards the west.

"Thanks," said Skelly, and then he turned to walk away. But then he paused and retraced his steps.

"By the way... what's that awful pong?" he asked. "It smells as though someone has dropped a stink bomb on the ground around here."

"Isn't it terrible!" said Blisterfoot. "It's been hanging around all day – that's why we're packing up and leaving."

"Oh, I see... I don't blame you! Thanks again," said Skelly, and he set off in the direction in which Blubberguts had previously pointed.

But Skelly had only walked for a short distance when he realised his mistake. "How stupid could I have been?" he mumbled under his breath. "It should have been obvious to me that the disgusting odour came from the creatures themselves because they were Rottanegs and, no doubt, up to no good."

After this revelation had suddenly dawned on him Skelly hurried back through the crowds, but the Rottanegs and their stall had already vanished – lock, stock and barrel... fortunately though, so had the smell! And this, of course, only confirmed his suspicions as to their identity.

After hunting high and low throughout the bazaar he still could not find his missing friend anywhere. Skelly feared the worst, for he knew the Rottanegs were renowned thieves, although he could not believe that they would really stoop as low as to count kidnapping amongst their many crimes. He shuddered at the very thought of it. The Rottanegs were known time bandits, therefore if they had kidnapped Amanda she could be anywhere at that very moment – possibly somewhere in the future or even in the past. The only thing Skelly could do now was to hope and pray that she would turn up safe and well again because he realised it was going to be a difficult (if not impossible) task to locate her whereabouts.

CHAPTER TEN

The Space Monster!

As it so happened, Amanda was still in the present for the time being. The Rottanegs had merely taken her to their secret hideaway where they were just about to remove the lid from her soundproof box.

Amanda felt very stupid at having been duped by the giant Rottaneg who had asked her to step into his office, especially after her mother had always drummed it into her that she should never go anywhere with strangers. But there was nothing that she could have done to prevent her capture anyway, because the Rottanegs had purposely come looking for her, and they could not believe their luck when she walked right up to her stall and played right into their hands. Regardless, the damage was already done and Amanda had suddenly found herself cooped-up in quite a large box. She tried in vain to escape from her prison but it was impossible, so, with nothing else to do, she curled up in a ball and went to sleep.

It was a smooth journey to the Rottanegs' hideaway and Amanda remained undisturbed until the lid was prized from the box. It was only then that she opened her eyes to be greeted by the three ugly faces of her captors staring in at her.

"Doesn't she look cute?" commented Bumblebutt with a ridiculous grin on his face. "It seems such a shame to disturb her."

"Oh, shut up you idiot," said Blubberguts, "and give me a hand to get her out of this box."

"Yes, let's have a good look at our treasure," Blisterfoot chipped in with an evil glint in his eye. Then he wrung his hands in eager anticipation as Amanda was plucked from the box.

"Get your grubby hands off me!" Amanda demanded of the big thug, whilst trying to shake free of his steel-like grip. "How dare you... Who do you think you are?"

"There's no need to be so rude," said Bumblebutt, feeling quite offended. "We are your new friends and we're not going to hurt you."

"If you were my friends, then you wouldn't be treating me like a prisoner," snapped Amanda angrily. "Why have you brought me here anyway?"

"This is your temporary home until we find a suitable owner for you," Blisterfoot said sneeringly.

"What do you mean?" Amanda asked in a frightened voice.

"There is a lucrative child-slave market out there and someone, somewhere in time, will pay dearly for a human child – especially a girl. We shall put you up for auction where you will eventually be sold to the highest bidder," the skinny Rottaneg gleefully told her.

Amanda felt terrified by now. What was she going to do, she wondered? She looked all around her, searching for a means of escape, but there seemed to be no way out. She did not even know where she was for that matter. It was quite a dark room with one or two candles on the walls that gave off an amber glow, and there were pipes and ducts running all over the place. It reminded her of the old boiler room at her school – and she was not supposed to go in there either!

As she resigned herself to a fate worse than death, tears welled up in Amanda's eyes and she began to cry. But, all of a sudden, her luck took a change for the better when her three captors unexpectedly let out a loud shriek and began to point at something behind Amanda, their fingers trembling as they shook in fear.

"Whatever is it?" asked Bumblebutt in a frightened voice.

"I'm not sure," answered Blisterfoot.

"I think it… it… it's a space monster," whimpered their big chief.

"*A SPACE MONSTER?!!*" yelled all three Rottanegs together.

"Waagh! Let's get out of here," they screamed. "Run for your lives."

Without any hesitation the Rottanegs scrambled out of a steel hatch in the roof, which clanged noisily when it slammed shut behind them, and then there was complete silence. Amanda had stopped crying as soon as she had witnessed the scene that had just taken place, before turning to stone as she watched the shadow on the walls growing larger in the flickering candlelight. Slowly, she turned around to see what manner of space monster it was that had been fearsome enough to frighten away the Rottanegs and was about to devour her.

But Amanda could not believe what she saw once she turned to confront the space monster, for perched on one of the pipes that ran along the wall was a large white rodent, his tiny shadow magnified 100-fold by the dull light of the flickering candle nearest to him.

"*BOGGLES!*" exclaimed Amanda, letting out a huge sigh of relief. "You're still alive!"

The white rat squinted his red, beady eyes in the direction of Amanda, while his long whiskers twitched frantically as he sniffed at the air.

"Amanda? Is that you?" asked Boggles in a squeaky voice. "Oh, yes, so it is… I can smell you now. I can't see very well, you see – it's these red eyes of mine, you know. I'm actually as blind as a rat… or should that be bat? No matter…"

"Goodness! I can understand you as well," gasped Amanda in complete astonishment. This device of Skelly's obviously works with animals too – how incredibly clever."

"Don't go away, I'll be down in just a mo," said Boggles.

"Like I'm going to go anywhere!" muttered Amanda.

True to his word, Boggles scurried along the wall pipe, slid down a vertical drainpipe and dropped gently onto her shoulder in what would be considered to be a mo in a rat's timescale.

"Boy, am I glad to see you," he said, busily nibbling away at her left ear while his whiskers brushed against Amanda's face.

"That tickles," she said with a chuckle.

"Oh, it really is so nice to see you again Amanda," squeaked Boggles between nibbles.

"It's nice to see you too Boggles. I'm so happy you survived your voyage into space – I was so worried about you."

"Phew! It was a bit of an adventure, I'm telling you," squeaked Boggles. "In a way it was quite exciting, actually. You see, I landed on Laktose as planned but then I couldn't get out of my space-egg. I sat there for three days with nothing to do except eat, so I scoffed all of my carrots… You haven't got any carrots on you now have you, perchance?"

Amanda shook her head.

"Sorry," she said, shrugging her shoulders, "but it's not the sort of thing I usually carry around with me."

"Pity," mumbled Boggles, "but never mind," and then he continued where he had left off. "…Anyway, along came these three ugly-looking things who picked up the space-egg and carried it away with 'em. Next, they dumped me and the space-egg in here but they hadn't got the intelligence to open up the cockpit and look inside. Well, as luck would have it, one of 'em knocked the release catch and I managed to get out of the cockpit. Since then I've been running about this place to my heart's content."

"I have to say that you certainly look well," remarked Amanda. "You must have found another supply of food after you ran out of carrots, or else you would probably have starved by now… What have you been eating?"

"Oh, that's another story," squeaked Boggles. "I'll have to show you though, because it'll take too long to explain."

"Do you know, I do believe the Rottanegs aren't coming back," said Amanda, momentarily changing the subject. "You scared them off good and proper. It was a stroke of luck that you came along when you did."

"Why don't you take a look out of that hatch they escaped through?" squeaked Boggles. "I've been wondering what's out there since I got here. I'm too small to be able to turn the wheel that opens it but I reckon you could do it quite easily."

Amanda agreed that it would be a good idea to find out where they were at least, so she grabbed hold of the steel wheel and turned it in a clockwise direction. The hatch made a clunking sound as it became unlocked and, using all the strength she could muster, Amanda pushed it open.

"Let me see… Let me see," repeated Boggles excitedly, at the same time jumping up and down on the spot.

Amanda obligingly lifted up the rat and placed him back onto her shoulder, whereupon they poked their heads out of the hatchway at the same moment. The hatch opened directly onto the surface of the planet but there was something really strange about its appearance: for one thing, it was pitch dark, as if it had been scorched by something really hot; and for another, there was no sign of life either. Not only that, but they were in deep space surrounded by darkness, with barely a star to be seen. Extraordinarily, the Milky Way was nowhere in sight! Amanda and Boggles exchanged puzzled glances, both of them raising their eyebrows in complete bewilderment.

"I don't think we're on the planet Rhom any more," said Amanda. "I wonder where we are… It's really weird out here."

"If you think this is weird, I'll show you something else that's even weirder," squeaked Boggles. "Come on – follow me."

Amanda closed the hatch behind her as Boggles bounded from her shoulder and led the way through a maze of corridors filled with pipework. After a while they arrived at what appeared to be an air-conditioning shaft that was just large enough for Amanda to squeeze into. Then, on her hands and knees, and in total darkness, she followed Boggles along the shaft for what seemed like an eternity. Eventually, she could see a tiny dot of light in the distance that became brighter and brighter as they moved towards it until, finally, they reached the entrance of the shaft.

The astonished girl gazed in awe at the scene before her, for here, in what must be the very heart of the planet, there was daylight! Also, the sky was coloured with several shades of mauves and pinks whilst the grass was greener than green; flowers bloomed all around and trees blossomed in all of their glory. Meanwhile, the sound of birds whistling merrily away in the treetops and hedgerows reached her ears – although they could not be seen – and pieces of coloured fabric that resembled butterflies fluttered silently by. It was bright and warm too, while, strangely enough, the sun shone although it was not even visible!

"There's daylight on the inside and night-time on the outside," said Amanda in a surprised voice. "It's almost as if the planet is inside out. And there's something missing too – there are no people here."

"I know," squeaked Boggles. "Isn't that great? I've been wandering around for three weeks now and I haven't seen a single soul; how pleasant it has been. And there's plenty to eat here too – the trees are full of fruit and I've even found a newly-planted carrot patch."

"Then there has to be people here," said Amanda. "I'm pretty sure the carrots wouldn't have planted themselves, so someone must have put them there."

"Well, I promise you that I haven't seen anyone. Mind you, I've heard voices, you know – whispering voices – and knocking sounds as well. It's quite spooky at times."

"Have you really? Where have you heard these sounds?" Amanda asked timidly, half expecting to hear them herself at any moment.

"Back where we came from," Boggles replied, "where the pipes are – and in that large chamber with the high ceiling we passed through on the way here."

"What chamber? I didn't see it; I was too busy trying to keep up with you. It's alright for you – you've got four legs and I've only got two. That means you can move twice as fast as me."

"Hmmm! I've never really given that any thought, but you could be right. However, you're much bigger than me so, in theory, you should be moving faster than me. Oh well, it doesn't really matter much – the point in question is the voices thing… I don't know how you failed to miss seeing the chamber. It's enormous, and stacked up to the ceiling with doors – big, black, iron doors. I thought it was only me that had poor eyesight."

"There's nothing wrong with my eyesight," Amanda retorted. "I was looking down at the floor, watching where I was going."

"Okay, point taken. Let's change the subject," Boggles suggested.

There was a moment's silence whilst Boggles and Amanda tried to think of another subject to talk about. Finally, Boggles came up with something.

"What have you done to your chin? I keep meaning to ask you why you're wearing a Band-Aid."

"I'm not supposed to tell anyone about it, but I think I can trust you. Besides, nobody else would be able to understand you anyway," said Amanda. "You see, it's not a real plaster – it's a speech converter in disguise. There is actually a miniscule transmitter and a receiver inserted into the padded part of the plaster... That's how I can understand what you're saying."

"Hmmm! I never gave that matter any thought either. I just took it for granted that you could understand me. What a clever idea, though. Who thought of it, your dad?"

"No, a friend of mine called Skelly lent it to me a couple of days ago. It was invented by a friend of his."

"You've got a friend up here in space? Wow! That's really cool. Is Skelly a pen pal? I wish I had a pen pal in space..."

"He's not a pen pal; he's a very close friend of mine. You'll like him. It's a long story how I met him and, in a round-about sort of way, he's the very reason how you ended up here too... I'll tell you about it some day. In the meantime, I can't get those voices out of my head. I think we should investigate the matter."

"*What! Are you nuts?*" exclaimed Boggles. "What if they're alien ghosts or something like that?"

"Stop it Boggles, you're frightening me! There's no such thing as ghosts, especially alien ghosts – or at least that's what

I'm going to keep telling myself. Anyway, even if they are ghosts they can't hurt you. I vote that we go in search of the voices. Are you with me?"

"I'll be right behind you all the way, Amanda," squeaked Boggles.

"No you won't, you little coward; you can go in front. I don't know where the chamber is but you do."

"Aw, you're such a bully at times, but if you insist. Let me just grab a couple of carrots before we go though, just to steady my nerves."

Boggles scurried away and disappeared over the grassy horizon. He returned a little later dragging behind him a large bunch of carrots and a small bunch of grapes.

"These are for you," he panted. "I thought you might be hungry."

"Thanks," said Amanda. "I see that you got the lion's share though!"

Regardless, Amanda was extremely hungry and she ate the grapes with gusto. When they had finished their brief snack the unlikely pair set off through the air conditioning duct as they went in search of the mysterious voices, with Boggles reluctantly leading the way.

CHAPTER ELEVEN

The Whispering Shylots

In no time at all, the intrepid duo arrived in a vast chamber. It always puzzled Amanda how it could take an age to get somewhere, yet the return journey was always quicker, especially when you did not particularly want to go back to a certain place.

Amanda shone her torch around the immense chamber. There was row upon row of black iron doors, just as Boggles had told her, stacked high above her. So high, in fact, that the powerful beam of light from her flashlight would not extend far enough to see where the rows ended. There must have been thousands of them – perhaps millions for that matter.

"You're right Boggles," said a stunned Amanda. "I really don't know how I missed seeing all of these doors."

"See – I told you so," Boggles said with a smug grin on his whiskery face. "There must be something wrong with your eyesight."

Amanda ignored Boggles' know-it-all attitude.

"I don't hear any voices, though," she said next.

"You have to encourage them," Boggles told her. "When I usually hear the voices they stop as soon as I arrive here, but I know this is where they come from. Let me show you how to make them happen."

Boggles grabbed a large carrot in his little pink paw and placed it into his mouth. Then he tapped three times on one of the pipes with it. A reply immediately came back as a tapping sound commenced. Amanda listened intently.

"Why, it's a distress signal!" she exclaimed. "Save Our Souls, they're saying. It's an SOS request – my dad taught it to me. If someone is in trouble the tapping is a code that is used to summon help."

Then the voices began.

"Help us… Let us out of here… We're trapped…" said the quiet, whispering voices that echoed eerily around the chamber.

"It is rather spooky, isn't it?" muttered Amanda. "Whoever they are must be behind those doors. But how can we release them?"

"Do you think we should release them?" asked Boggles. "I mean, they could be baddies and we'll be right back where we started."

"I don't think they're baddies; their voices seem far too soft and gentle," Amanda replied.

"Hmmm!" grunted Boggles. "I don't know how you can tell, but I trust your judgement. If you really think we should set them free there's a lever over there that has a label on it saying 'DOOR RELEASE' – I spotted it just the other day. I can't reach it though, because I'm too small, so you'll have to operate it. And, I just want you to know, that I really am right behind you on this one!"

Boggles showed Amanda where the lever was located and Amanda took a deep breath.

"Well, here goes," she said. "Let's see what's behind those doors."

She pulled down on the lever using all of her strength and it began to move slowly with a horrible grating sound, the sort that put her teeth on edge. This was followed by a loud clunking noise as the catches became free and the black cast-iron doors creaked fully open. There was a series of relieved "Oohs" and "Aahs" that came from behind the doors and then a chorus of "*We're free!*" reverberated eerily around the room. Ghostly figures immediately began to appear in the doorways – blue-grey in colour and almost transparent, their robes flowing gently in a breeze that did not even exist – figures who stood and stared down upon Amanda and Boggles.

"They… they are ghosts," gasped Boggles in dismay, his knees knocking together as he trembled in terror. "I told you so… What have you done Amanda?"

"Don't be silly Boggles; ghosts don't talk," said Amanda. "Pull yourself together for goodness sake – they're not going to harm us."

By this time the whispering figures had began to descend to ground level, making not a single sound as they floated gently downwards, where they now huddled together in large groups eyeing Amanda and Boggles with a mixture of awe and reverence. When they had all safely congregated on the ground there was a hushed silence.

"Hi! I'm Amanda… and this is my friend Boggles the rat. We've just set you free."

"Don't bring me into this," squeaked Boggles.

"Shut up Boggles and show them that you're friendly."

Boggles peered out from behind Amanda's legs where he had been cowering away. He bared his teeth in an attempt at a smile. There followed a frightened intake of breath from the thousands of figures who had misinterpreted Boggles' smile as a threatening snarl, and they retreated slightly, huddling ever-closer together.

"Oh, don't worry about him," Amanda reassured them. "He's only a tame rat – he won't harm you. In fact, he's more afraid of you."

"*Amanda!*" squealed Boggles. "You're embarrassing me!"

"You're embarrassing yourself, you numbskull. Come up here on my shoulder and stop being such a baby," snapped Amanda.

Boggles did as he was told and Amanda continued to address the crowd.

"We're from the planet Earth and we came here quite by accident really, after being captured by the Rottanegs," she announced. "What a beautiful planet you have here… even if it is inside out!"

One of the figures took a step towards Amanda. She was very beautiful, with thin, chiselled features, as if she was a statue carved from stone, and she had huge almond-shaped eyes that blinked slowly when they rolled about her face.

"Thank you…" said the figure in a soft whisper. "Thank you for appreciating our planet, and thank you for setting us free."

"Who are you?" asked Amanda, "and how did you become to be trapped behind those doors?"

"We are an ancient race of Milkunians known as The Whispering Shylots," replied the female. "I am Princess Jenta-

Lee, the spokeswoman. We too were captured by the Rottanegs who imprisoned us in these cells. They crash-landed onto our planet, embedding their time machine deep into the surface, threatening us that if we didn't do as we were told they would turn us into a freak show and parade our people in front of an audience. We are a bashful nation; therefore we could not allow them to do that, for it is not in our nature to be outgoing."

"I see," said Amanda.

Princess Jenta-Lee went on to explain that their planet was a small star which had burnt out many light years ago, and it belonged in the galaxy of the Milky Way. It was a pole star that formerly held prime position at the north end of the galaxy, illuminating the path for star sailors, just like a lighthouse warns mariners of underlying rocks in an ocean. The Rottanegs had used their time-machine to drag the entire planet through a black hole, scorching the surface because it was such a tight squeeze, and replacing it in deepest, darkest space several light years away from the Milky Way so they could use it as a hideaway. This particular area they had been brought to was a no-man's land known as The Waste of Space and they did not belong there at all.

After Princess Jenta-Lee had finished explaining their dilemma, Amanda and Boggles were then led from the gloomy depths of the time-machine, back through the air-conditioning duct, and taken to the planet's inner core where beauty prevailed and life flourished. The Shylots flocked there in their thousands, pleased to be allowed the freedom to roam their land once more.

They were such an easy-going, mild-mannered race of people and Amanda was in complete awe of them. She also marvelled at her hosts' deportment: Princess Jenta-Lee and her entourage carried their tall forms in an elegant and graceful style, the likes of which she had never seen before, with their heads aloft and their slender bodies erect. All of the women were truly beautiful and the men were strikingly handsome, their children bearing the same mannerisms that would be their hallmark as they developed into adulthood. How she wished that she could help these people to regain their rightful place at the head of the Milky Way. If anyone deserved justice, then they certainly did, she thought. As she pondered over this, all of a sudden Amanda had a brainwave, so she approached Princess Jenta-Lee to put forward her suggestion.

"All is not lost," she gabbled excitedly. "I think we can help you because we have a time-machine in our possession."

"But nobody knows how to operate it," said Princess Jenta-Lee.

"No, I'm not talking about the massive one that belongs to the Rottanegs... We – meaning Boggles and I – have a miniature space-egg that can fly through time. I am too big to fit into it but Boggles can fly it."

"Oh, no!" squeaked Boggles. "I'm not getting into that thing again. Look what happened to me the last time I got into it."

"What did he say?" asked Princess Jenta-Lee, for all she could hear was a series of whinging squeaks.

"He said that he'd love to help out," grinned Amanda. "The miniature space-egg won't be powerful enough to move your planet, but the co-ordinates are already programmed in to fly to

Laktose, so we can send him to find our friend Captain Skelly – He'll know what to do."

"Thanks for nothing," groaned Boggles. "I thought you were my friend."

"I am your friend, and you're supposed to be my friend, and this is what friends do when they're in trouble – they help each other out," Amanda told Boggles, adamant that she would be able to convince him.

"Oh, very well then… But just this once," agreed Boggles.

Having explained to Princess Jenta-Lee exactly who Skelly was, they set out to seek the whereabouts of the space-egg and found it tucked away in the junk room of the Rottanegs' own time-machine. Luckily, it had not been damaged following the ill-treatment it had received during its many moves and, after a major dusting down, the tiny space-egg was ready to fly to Laktose. Following a tearful farewell from Boggles, whereupon Amanda reassured him that he would only be gone for a short time, he was successfully launched on his rescue mission with a note addressed to Skelly, briefly explaining the predicament the Whispering Shylots were in.

The note read thus:

Dear Skelly,

I hope you are well. We are in a spot of bother at present; however, I am okay. Please send help to relocate the ancient race of Shylots.

This is Boggles: he is a white lab rat who is quite a pleasant little chap although he can be a bit of a wimp at times – just ignore his moaning ways… He will explain what has happened

112

but you need to wear the spare speech converter to understand him – it works on animals too! See you soon.

Luv, Amanda.

Amanda was true to her word. Within a day of Boggles' departure, Skelly arrived with a squadron of space-eggs containing a team of top Flight Engineers from Laktose. They were greeted quietly by the Shylots who were not prone to showing any excitement, although they were no doubt jumping for joy inside their own minds. Boggles was proudly given the task of being Skelly's co-pilot for the return journey to the Shylots' planet, travelling in a brand-new, dual-controlled, state-of-the-art space-egg.

The team of specialist engineers quickly got to work on the Rottanegs' giant time-machine that was securely attached to the planet with four space anchors. Having read the time-machine's instruction manual from cover to cover, the team were soon convinced that the planet was ready to be moved and the huge operation thus began. Very soon, the planet was safely back in its true position at the north end of its galaxy and, after a little precision re-alignment of the planet, the Rottanegs' time-machine was excavated from the surface before being towed away by six Laktosian recovery freighters. It was later impounded by the Inter-Galactic Customs and Excise Authorities, who had a momentous task ahead of them as they sorted out several centuries of loot and treasure which the thieving time bandits had collected.

Skelly explained to Amanda that without their time-machine the Rottanegs had no future – or past for that matter! The three nasty Rottanegs had hurriedly fled in a life-raft capsule and they would, at the present time, be floating around helplessly, somewhere in space. Eventually, the three thugs would be picked up by an Inter-Galactic Space Cruiser Patrol and brought to justice.

The time had now come for Amanda to say goodbye to the Whispering Shylots. Because they were such a quiet and reserved race of people, not a lot of fuss was made of her departure; therefore, Amanda left the planet after only a brief farewell. However, she did not leave empty-handed. As a way of showing her peoples' gratitude for saving their race and their planet from disaster, Princess Jenta-Lee presented Amanda with a precious jewel-encrusted brooch in the shape of a dove of peace, which also displayed her name beneath it. And Boggles was given a huge crate of carrots that would see him through the remainder of his stay in outer-space. Afterwards, Princess Jenta-Lee bid them a fond farewell, with an open invitation for everyone involved in the rescue mission to visit their harmonious planet whenever they wished.

CHAPTER TWELVE

King Sizemars' Party

Upon her return to Laktose, Amanda found herself back in the now familiar room on the top floor of The Ocean View Hotel, whilst Boggles was given a room of his own on the next level. The smallest floating bed on the planet was soon located and thus delivered to the hotel for Boggles to while away his sleeping hours in comfort – and sleeping was something that he seemed to enjoy doing most. He was now the biggest talking point on the planet. Not only had the Laktosians got a giant human child in their midst, but there was also a strange creature known as a rat, something they had never seen nor heard of before. It was quite an important event to have two weird aliens on their planet and the pair of celebrities were treated like royalty. Everywhere Amanda and Boggles went people stared, pointed, waved, shook hands (and paws) and even bowed to them.

Amanda had quickly become used to her celebrity status, taking it all in her stride, although the fuss she was getting still made her feel like a special person. Boggles, on the other hand, was lapping up the attention, taking advantage of every opportunity he could to be in the limelight. The famous duo were constantly in great demand: they were plastered all over the planet's newspaper, interviewed on radio shows, and there were even star guest appearances on television too.

Of course, Amanda had to translate to the audiences whatever Boggles said and during one television appearance the presenter asked Boggles how he came by such an unusual name.

"Oh, it was given to me by a very dear friend of mine on Earth," he said, "Amanda's father to be exact... But it's not my real name you know."

"What is your real name?" asked the presenter.

"My real name is Reginald," Boggles proudly announced.

"*Reginald!*" exclaimed Amanda in surprise.

"What's wrong with my name then?" asked Boggles indignantly.

"You don't look like a Reginald to me – Do you have a last name as well?"

"Of course I do – It's Rat," squeaked Boggles.

Amanda burst out laughing.

"Reginald Rat, eh? I've heard it all now. I never would have guessed."

"Well, you never asked, did you?"

"I thought your real name was Boggles, just plain and simple Boggles. I'm still going to call you Boggles though, because that's how I've always known you," said Amanda.

"That's fine," squeaked Boggles. "I prefer to be called Boggles anyway. I never did like the name Reginald."

And that was how the enlightening interview ended.

But the climax of their celebrity lifestyle was yet to come. King Sizemars sent an invitation for Amanda and Boggles to attend an informal dinner at his palace on the mound, where they

116

would be special guests of honour. The invitation requested that neither of them gave mention to anyone that they were going to the palace, for it was intended to be a quiet affair and the king did not want the press to get wind of it. Amanda was so excited and she was longing to tell Skelly all about her important invitation, but she remained faithful to the king and never mentioned a word about it.

On the evening of the quiet dinner party Amanda and Boggles prepared themselves for their audience with the king. Amanda did not want to draw attention to herself by wearing fancy clothes which were likely to cause people to ask her where she was going, so she dressed in casual jeans and her favourite denim jacket, wearing a colourful tie-dyed T-shirt beneath it. Then she took the Supa-Tube elevator to the ground floor. Although it was a bit of a squeeze, Boggles shared the lift with her because he was too tiny to travel in one of the capsules alone. When they stepped outside the hotel there was not a soul to be seen. The city's streets were unusually deserted. This took Amanda completely by surprise for it was still early evening and Laktosian people did not normally go to bed until the last planet had gone down over the horizon.

Before she had a chance to ponder too deeply over this, a large hover-cruiser suddenly appeared out of thin air. The white, stretched Laktosine with black tinted windows stopped right in front of her and its invisible doors immediately appeared in order to allow her and Boggles entry.

"Are you taking us to the palace?" Amanda asked the driver before stepping into the vehicle.

"Yes," came the rather abrupt reply from the chauffeur.

So Amanda climbed aboard with Boggles clinging tightly to her shoulders.

"Make yourselves comfortable," mumbled the chauffeur in a voice that was difficult to understand. He did not even turn around to look at them when he spoke. Instead, he sat hunched over the controls with his hat tilted forwards and dark sunglasses hiding his eyes from view.

Once they had seated themselves down, Amanda and Boggles were whisked briskly away and, in no time at all, they arrived at the palace on the mound. The doors of the Laktosine materialised, again as if by magic, and Amanda stepped out with Boggles firmly perched upon her shoulders. The hunched figure of the chauffeur then led them up a long flight of stairs to the grand entrance of the palace. Amanda had counted 350 steps by the time she reached the veranda that surrounded the lofty entrance of the palace and she was quite out of breath. When they got to the veranda, the mysterious chauffeur then touched the outer wall of the palace and an invisible door instantly appeared.

At that moment a fanfare of trumpets sounded and a red carpet rolled rapidly towards them along a lengthy hallway, unfurling itself fully when it stopped at their feet. Hordes of people suddenly began to appear from behind tiers of pillars that lined either side of the hallway, clapping and cheering as they emerged from their hiding places. The chauffeur had removed his hat and sunglasses by this time and, no longer hunched up, he was standing upright.

"*SKELLY!*" exclaimed Amanda in delight.

"Hi Amanda," he said, beaming all over his face.

"Why the disguise?" she asked.

"Because this is a Laktosian party especially for you and Boggles, so we wanted it to be a complete surprise... You are the guests of honour, you see."

Amanda was overwhelmed and all she could say was: "Cool!"

"Come along," said Skelly. "The king is waiting for you at the other end of the hall, so we had better not keep him waiting."

Skelly proudly marched Amanda along the red carpet, amidst the grinning, cheering Laktosian crowd, until they came face to face with the king. Instantly, the crowd fell silent.

"Welcome to my palace," said King Sizemars. "My home is your home too. I have been hearing splendid things about the pair of you. You have discovered the whereabouts of the Lost Planet of Ancient Laktosians and it has now been repositioned in its rightful place; therefore, we are eternally grateful to you... We, the Laktosians, wish to bestow upon you the highest award available in the entire galaxy of the Milky Way – The Gold Star of Curdisland – a cherished precious metal made of 100-carat milky-white gold, and the only one of its kind in existence."

Amanda looked at the bright, shiny piece of jewellery in amazement.

"Oh, it was nothing," she gasped. "But thank you anyway. What a beautiful piece of jewellery... and 100-carats too!"

"*100 carrots!*" squeaked Boggles in delight. "They're giving us 100 carrots? I can't wait."

"No, Boggles – it's a form of measurement. Gold is weighed in carats, not carrots... King Sizemars is giving us this gold star."

"Can you eat it?" asked Boggles.

"No, of course not!"

"Oh, how boring," yawned Boggles.

"It's very valuable, you know – much more valuable than carrots," Amanda told Boggles. "We can't possibly accept it though, King Sizemars..."

"Yes we can," Boggles interrupted. "Think how many carrots we can get in exchange."

"Shut up Boggles and say thank you to the king. I don't know what's happened to your manners since you became famous."

"Sorree!" Boggles sarcastically muttered. "Er...Thank you King Sizemars," he squeaked.

But no-one understood him except for Amanda and Skelly.

"That's much better," said Amanda. "Now, where was I? Oh yes... We can't accept the Gold Star of Curdisland because we would be afraid of losing it, so we think it will be much safer on your planet."

"Very well," agreed the king, "but it is now yours and you can come and claim it whenever you wish. Also, we would like to offer you the freedom of the city of Kallseum where you may come and go as you please."

"Thank you again," said Amanda.

"Yes, thank you," squeaked Boggles, and still nobody understood him.

"Right, now that the formalities are out of the way – let's party!" shrieked the king at the top of his voice.

There was a roar of delight from the crowd and they immediately surged towards the banqueting room. The walls of the banqueting room were covered with murals of famous Laktosian people throughout history and King Sizemars explained that a painting of Skelly, Amanda and Boggles would soon be added to it.

The entire population of the planet Laktose had turned out to attend the party of the year, just as they had done for Skelly's award party during the previous year, which explained the absence of people on the streets of Kallseum. Skelly's parents were pleased to see Amanda again and so too were all the friends she had made during her stay at the Mountain Lodge Resort whilst mountain surfing. The Shylots had declined their invitation to attend but Amanda understood their reason for this. However, they sent a telegram congratulating Amanda and Boggles, wishing them all the best for the future, the past and the present.

After the feast a dance was held in the grand ballroom of the palace. It was a disco, in fact, with a live band called The Milkmen who played music from different ages throughout time. They were quite an extraordinary act because they did not have any musical instruments at all. Instead, they made the sound of electric guitars, drums, synthesizers and just about every type of instrument known, with the use of their vocal chords. It was certainly different but very entertaining indeed. And there was also another attraction that provided a bizarre visual effect.

When Skelly had returned to his home planet he had introduced his own brand of multi-coloured, flavoured milkshakes to the Laktosian public, adding several new shades to the range. So, as people danced to the live band they supped at the popular milkshakes, their flesh changing colour as they tried different flavours – It was just as though flashing disco lights had been set up at the venue. Not only did the dancers change colour, but they constantly changed their flexible bodies into a variety of shapes, thus adding even more excitement to the already spectacular floor show.

Amanda joined in the celebrating too. She clapped her hands in time to the music, stamped her feet and grinned from ear to ear while watching everyone having such fun. She was so popular that everybody wanted to dance with her, and she was quickly swept away by the tide of party-goers. Amanda danced with Skelly, Mr. and Mrs. Jelly, and several times with King Sizemars until, eventually, she could no longer stand up. By this time though, the evening had come to an abrupt end as the people of Laktose all went home to bed at their usual hour.

Boggles had spent the entire evening in the palace kitchen, happily scoffing away at a hamper of carrots that had been provided especially for him. He was not particularly keen on loud music, and he had never been much of a dancer, so he was quite content with his lot.

Amanda, Boggles and Skelly were given accommodation at the palace for the night, where a suite of rooms that took up an entire floor had been prepared for the special guests in the most luxurious of surroundings. At the end of the night they fell into their floating four-poster beds, completely and utterly exhausted, having experienced the most wonderful evening of their lives... thus ended the party of the year for the very important guests of honour, and everyone else on Laktose too.

CHAPTER THIRTEEN

Farewell to Laktose

It was the day after the memorable palace party. Amanda awoke early, her ears still ringing from the noisy send-off that the Laktosians had given her. Bleary-eyed and remaining in her dreamlike state of mind, she looked out of the bedroom window. She had arisen just in time to witness the surrounding planets begin their daily orbit – a sight that she would never have wanted to miss for the world.

The palace was located on the mound at the head of the city and held the most prominent position, where it overlooked the whole city and the ocean beyond. The green light of dawn was becoming brighter all of the while, changing the colours of the Sea of Milk from a shade of jade green to its daytime pastel hue. Amanda stood for a while to marvel at the beauty of daybreak on Laktose, which caused every colour of the rainbow to reflect on the unique, dome-shaped dwellings that filled the valley and formed the city of Kallseum. Then she reached for her camera and took some more snapshots for her dad's photo album.

And when she thought about her father Amanda came down to Earth with a bump, for today she would be returning home. In a way she was happy to be going home, yet, on the other hand, she was also sad to be leaving. This had to be the most unforgettable summer vacation she had ever taken and time had simply flown by. Amanda had only seen a fraction of the Milky Way and there was so much more that remained to be discovered, but there simply was not enough time to cram everything in.

All of a sudden, Amanda's thoughts were disturbed by the sound of squealing... Boggles appeared to be in trouble! As fast as lightning, she rushed into Boggles' bedroom where she discovered that his pitiful squeals were coming from beneath a large pile of carrots.

"*BOGGLES!*" Amanda yelled. "Boggles... come out of there".

The pile of carrots began to move and then a familiar-looking, white, pointed face emerged amidst the orange heap, its whiskers twitching away like a plate of jelly in an earthquake.

"What on Earth has got into you?" asked Amanda in total surprise.

"Oh... Oh... I must have been dreaming," came the pathetic, squeaky reply. "I dreamt that I was being attacked by a vicious gang of killer carrots."

"What a ridiculous dream! How did that pile of carrots get to be on top of you in the first place?"

"Well, I built a model out of them," Boggles sleepily explained. "It was an exact replica of the palace, and I built it on that shelf above me – I couldn't sleep last night, you see, so I had to find something to do – The whole thing must have collapsed in on me during the night."

"You silly animal," laughed Amanda, as she pulled him from the pile of carrots. "I can't imagine a palace built of carrots, and I certainly can't imagine that it would stay up for long either... You are funny."

Amanda picked up Boggles and kissed him lovingly on the tip of his tiny pink nose. "Why couldn't you sleep?" she asked.

"I don't want to go home," he whimpered.

"Me neither," agreed Amanda, "but we have to. I shall really miss everyone here, but I miss my parents and my friends as well and I would dearly like to see them again."

"Oh no, it's not that," said Boggles.

Amanda looked at him with a puzzled expression on her face.

"Then what is it?" she asked.

"I... I... I'm afraid of flying," he admitted shamefully.

"Oh, you poor thing! Don't worry, you'll be okay. Hold on a moment though... you're supposed to be a test pilot, aren't you? You made it here safely, so what's the problem?"

"Yes, but only just," Boggles whimpered. "It's no good trying to fool myself – I know I'm not really a test pilot. I'm not stupid you know; I do realise that your father used me as a guinea-pig in order to test out his precious space-egg."

"You're not a guinea-pig, you're a rat!" Amanda said with a laugh, trying to make light of the situation and put Boggles' mind at ease.

"Oh, ha-ha! Very funny!" squeaked Boggles angrily. "Do you mind? This is a sensitive issue."

"You'll be fine – stop being such a wimp," said Amanda. "Pull yourself together... Come along now, let's go and find Skelly."

But, even though Amanda had shrugged off Boggles' fear of flying, she was still concerned for him all the same.

When they eventually found Skelly, he was in the dining room with King Sizemars. They swiftly rose to their feet when Amanda and Boggles entered the room.

"You're just in time," said the king, who seemed to be in rather a jovial mood. "Breakfast is about to be served. There's nothing like a hearty breakfast to set you up for the day."

But nobody was really in the mood for eating because everybody felt saddened by the impending departure, and the whole assembly pushed their food lazily around their plates. Boggles did not even eat a single scrap of food, which was most unusual for him. From this, King Sizemars deduced that something else was amiss too.

"What's wrong with your friend the rat?" he whispered to Amanda.

"He doesn't want to fly," Amanda replied.

"The poor little chap's lost his nerve has he? Oh dear, how's he going to get home then? There is no alternative but to fly."

"There's no need to whisper; I can hear you talking about me, you know… It's not that I don't want to fly – I'm actually afraid of flying," Boggles owned up bravely. "It's not so bad if you're with someone, but flying that space-egg on my own is a horribly frightening thought."

"You don't have to worry about flying alone," Skelly told Boggles. "You can fly in Amanda's space-egg with her. We've decided to give you a brand-new, state-of-the-art, modern space-egg – just like mine – as a leaving present. The one you've got is so outdated, it's unreal. In fact, it really belongs in a museum nowadays."

"But you had the same type of space-egg as ours when you came to Earth," Amanda remarked.

"Yes, but I crash-landed on Earth donkey's years ago; technology has moved on since then."

Amanda frowned worriedly.

"Sorry Skelly – We really can't accept the modern space-egg..."

"Yes, we can," interrupted Boggles, delighted at the thought of not having to travel alone.

"Quiet, Boggles," warned Amanda.

Boggles did as he was told and fell silent.

"Why not?" asked Skelly.

"Because it's my dad's pride and joy; he'd never forgive me if I didn't return his old space-egg to him."

"So we can't tempt you with a new one?"

"No!" Amanda flatly said.

"Oh, well – maybe another time then. I'm sure your dad will want an up-to-date version at some time in the future, especially when he sees my new one... Luckily, we've already prepared your old space-egg for flight because I had a feeling you would turn down our offer."

Amanda's eyes lit up, whilst Boggles began to groan in dismay.

"Although," added Skelly, "we've made a few slight alterations. For instance: the communications system had had it, so we've installed a more advanced one and you will now be able to talk to your dad as soon as you leave the Milky Way."

Amanda clasped her hands together gleefully.

"And," Skelly continued, "the miniature space-egg is now attached to the larger one – piggy-back style, so to speak, a bit like that space shuttle thingy on your planet, or a luggage carrier on a car roof – therefore, Boggles will be able to accompany you after all."

"Yippee!" squeaked Boggles as he jumped for joy. "Let's stock it up with carrots now."

"I think you should lay off the carrots for a while, they're playing havoc with your mind," Amanda told him.

"Not to mention my insides – I've got terrible wind lately," Boggles informed her.

"*Great!*" snorted Amanda. "Now I really can't wait to travel home with you in such a confined space."

Accompanied by Skelly and King Sizemars, Amanda and Boggles travelled in the Laktosine to their point of departure. At the egg-port they were greeted by droves of people: the whole population of the planet had turned out to see them off and they were still partying, drinking gallons of coloured milkshakes as if they were going out of fashion.

"I will make this an official celebration to commemorate your visit to Laktose," announced King Sizemars. "This date in our lunar calendar will become known as 'Big Am and Little Bog Day' from this moment on."

"Thank you," said Amanda. "Speaking on behalf of the two of us, we are both flattered by the gesture."

"No, thank you," replied King Sizemars. "It has been a joy to meet your acquaintance; therefore, the pleasure is all mine."

With that, he bent forward and kissed Amanda's hand, at the same time bowing low to the ground.

"And thank you also, Boggles. I can't understand a word that you say and you're a little weird at times but you've been great fun," said King Sizemars as he reached down and shook all four of his tiny pink paws.

"What'd he say?" asked Boggles.

"I'll tell you later," said Amanda.

"Captain Skelly will escort you from our galaxy," said King Sizemars. "Have a safe journey home."

Then the king retired to his royal box to watch their departure.

"I'll miss you Amanda," said Skelly. "It's been lovely to see you again, and such a nice surprise."

"I'll miss you too Skelly... Will you be visiting Earth again in the near future?"

"Most definitely," he replied. "I'll be seeing you very soon."

They hugged each other fondly before stepping towards their waiting space-eggs.

"Hey! What about me?" squeaked Boggles.

"Yes, I guess I'll miss you too," laughed Skelly. "You're quite a character and I'm pretty sure that I'm going to be seeing more of you in the future."

Skelly held out his hand and shook Boggles warmly by the paw.

"I'll miss you as well Amanda," squeaked Boggles.

"You're coming with me, you fool!" Amanda said, rather despairingly.

"Oh, yes – silly me," said Boggles. "I had forgotten."

"Too busy thinking about carrots I expect," Amanda said with a chuckle. "Come along now Boggles – get inside the space-egg."

The people of Laktose watched the countdown in tense anticipation as the coloured sand from the giant-sized, glass egg-timer poured from the top section, until the bottom half was full. Then, with a loud whooshing sound Amanda, Boggles and Skelly were all airborne. Amanda glanced down at Laktose as it quickly became a tiny dot far behind her, mingling in with the billions of other planets in the star system so that she could not even tell them apart. Flying side by side, in no time at all the space-eggs swept across the Milky Way until they came to the Whispering Shylots' planet, which was now re-emitting its luxurious, radiant glow that marked the start (or the end – whichever way you look at it) of the galaxy. At this point of the journey, Skelly waved to his companions before peeling off and returning home. From that moment on, Amanda and Boggles were alone in space.

CHAPTER FOURTEEN

Caught by the Fish… er… Men?

"We should be approaching a black hole shortly, which is the stargate to our own galaxy," said Amanda.

Boggles didn't reply. Instead, all she heard was a loud snore.

"Typical!" she muttered. "Just when I wanted someone to talk to, he decides to fall asleep… Oh, there it is!"

Amanda had spotted the black hole, or so she thought.

"That's funny though," she mumbled again as she continued to talk to herself. "What's it doing over there? I don't understand, because the space-egg is programmed to head directly towards it, but it's not where it is supposed to be. Oh, well…"

Amanda quickly grabbed hold of the controls and swung the space-egg to her left as she began to alter course. After that, just as the space-egg was about to enter the mouth of the black hole, Amanda pressed the green button that would rocket her through hyperspace and back to her own galaxy. But, instead of the awesome power surge she was expecting, quite the opposite happened: the space-egg began to slow down until it spluttered and stopped altogether. Amanda rapidly became worried. The ride was already beginning to become bumpy because they were entering the black hole, and now she had lost all of the engine power as well – the very thing that was needed to accelerate through it. She pushed the green button again and this time the entire electrical system failed. At that moment, Boggles awoke and opened his eyes.

"Aagh! I've gone blind… I've gone blind!" he shrieked.

"The lights have gone out," Amanda told him.

"I don't care, Amanda – I've gone blind," Boggles repeated.

"*No, you idiot!* The lights have gone out because the electrics have failed – In other words, we've broken down," Amanda informed him, trying hard to remain calm.

"Phew! Thank goodness for that; for one terrible moment I really thought I had lost my eyesight… Where are you? I still can't see you."

"I'm right next to you, and I can't see you either."

"Don't leave me will you?"

"Where am I going to go, for pity's sake?"

"Where are my carrots? I need a carrot."

"What is this, Twenty Questions? You're not having a carrot now… I won't be able to stand the noise of you crunching away on a carrot while we sit here in the dark; it will be so annoying."

"But I need a carrot – they help me to see in the dark."

"If I hear another word about carrots I'll take one and poke it in your eye, then you definitely won't be able to see anything!" Amanda told him.

She was at the end of her tether because she did not know what to do, and Boggles was beginning to irritate her.

Meanwhile, the space-egg was being tossed around and they were being flung about like rag dolls.

"I feel sea-sick," groaned Boggles.

"Air-sick or space-sick," Amanda corrected him.

"Whatever! I just don't feel well," he whimpered.

"I'm sorry you don't feel well but there's nothing I can do about it," said Amanda. "If it's any consolation, I don't exactly feel particularly brilliant myself."

At the very moment she had finished saying her sentence the space-egg unexpectedly began to become more stable. They were not being tossed around any more and it felt as if they were bobbing up and down in the gentle swell of an ocean.

"Is it my imagination, or is the black hole moving away?" asked Boggles, finally finding something more constructive to say.

"It certainly appears to be," Amanda agreed in surprise. "That's odd though, because we can't have passed through it in such a short time, especially with no power."

"Yep, it's definitely going – Look!" said Boggles as he pointed to the black hole that was becoming smaller and smaller.

"Either that or we're drifting away from it," said Amanda. "It's hard to tell with it being so dark."

For the next few minutes they watched in silent astonishment until the black hole had disappeared altogether, by which time the space-egg had completely steadied itself. Everything was then calm, including Amanda and Boggles; however, they were rapidly becoming depressed by their dark surroundings.

"I wonder where we are," Amanda said dismally. "There's nothing at all that can be seen – no stars, no planets – nothing!"

"We could be marooned here forever," Boggles squeaked in a gloomy voice. "We've no electrics, no communications system – who's going to help us now? We're doomed... we're doomed..."

"We're drifting helplessly in space. If only someone would throw us a lifeline," Amanda went on.

All of a sudden their prayers were answered when a light appeared behind them, growing stronger and brighter all of the time; and the powerful beam of the spotlight moved this way and that, as if it was looking for something. Eventually, it picked up the space-egg in its strong ray of light. After focussing on the stricken craft for a short period of time, the beam of light moved away, scanning the dark void of space ahead of it as it continued to search for whatever it was searching for. The searchlight had to be attached to something, thought Amanda, and, sure enough, it was: Amanda and Boggles watched in stunned silence whilst an enormous vessel passed quietly overhead with a long, dangly thing trailing beneath it.

"What do you think it is?" asked Boggles.

"It looks like a ship," said Amanda. "An ocean-going ship! But it can't be... we're in space!"

"It could be a spaceship though," Boggles announced confidently.

"And it's got what looks like the hose of a giant vacuum cleaner attached beneath it too," said the flabbergasted girl.

It seemed to take an age for the massive ship to pass overhead but it finally cleared the space-egg and began to move away.

"They didn't see us," wailed Boggles in dismay. "There might never be anyone else coming this way ever again."

"Hey! We're down here," yelled Amanda at the top of her voice, and then added: "...As if they are going to be able to hear us."

The forlorn pair immediately slipped back into a despondent mood, but then, without warning, a loud clanging sound nearly caused them to jump out of their skins.

"What on Earth?" said Amanda and Boggles at precisely the same moment.

"So, they did see us after all," Boggles squeaked gleefully. "Look, Amanda – there's something attached to our space-egg and we're being dragged towards that giant ship."

Amanda glanced out of the glass cockpit and noticed the sturdy line that was reeling them in.

"Yes, I see it," she said. "Let's just hope that whoever is rescuing us is going to be friendly."

Meanwhile, on board the vast spaceship, the crew were busy hauling in their latest catch.

"Heave-ho me hearties," said the Captain in a rich, deep voice. "Let's have it up here on the main deck and see what we've caught in our mag-net."

"Looks like we've got a giant clam, Skipper," said one of the deckhands.

"You've been reading too many books about mariners, m'lad – there's no such thing as clams up here in space….Move aside and let me have a look-see."

The deckhands moved away from their catch so that the skipper could take a peek.

"Mother of Pearl!" exclaimed the skipper. "I ain't seen one of these in many a light year."

"Then it is a giant clam," said the same deckhand who made the earlier comment.

"No – ain't you be listening to me Guppy? It's not a giant clam; it's a space-egg – a Laktosian space-egg at that – with a miniature one attached to it like a limpet."

I've never seen one before Skipper," said Guppy.

"Ya won't have – as rare as hens' teeth they are. S'most unusual to find one dumped here in space. In fact, in all me years as an Inter-Galactic Space Captain, I ain't never seen one scrapped. It's not damaged, neither, so my guess is there's something fishy about the reason for it being here. I think we should open it up and have a look inside… There should be a clasp around here somewhere that opens up the cockpit," said the Captain, as he bent down and began to fish around.

Until that moment, Amanda and Boggles had sat quietly in the interior of their space-egg, looking at the several pairs of legs that were visible through the smoked glass, because that was all they could see. And, of course, they could not hear the conversation either. So, when the Captain bent down to release the clasp that secured the hatch, both of them had the shock of their lives, for they could see that he had the head of a fish!

However, the Captain and his crew seemed to be equally as shocked when the cockpit was opened.

"Great Jumping Catfish!" he exclaimed. "What manner of creatures are these? They're definitely not Laktosian."

Amanda and Boggles stared at the Captain and his crew with their mouths wide open, because the entire gathering had the bodies of men and the heads of fish... assorted species of fish too. But, after getting over her initial shock, Amanda finally managed to speak.

"Hi, I'm Amanda," she said. "I'm a human being... And this is my friend Boggles – he's a white lab rat."

"Holy scrap merchants!" gasped the second mate. "They make a weird sound too."

"Can we eat them?" asked one of the deckhands, who had the head of a mackerel.

"No, of course you can't eat us!" Amanda retorted rather indignantly. "For a start, my mum and dad wouldn't be at all pleased if you did; and, for another thing, I wouldn't taste at all nice."

"What about that thing then?" said the mackerel, pointing at Boggles.

"You wouldn't like the taste of him either – He eats too many carrots," Amanda told the fishy-looking man.

"What'd he say?" asked Boggles, who was only understanding Amanda's side of the conversation.

"I don't think you want to know what he said," Amanda replied.

"Well, said the Captain, scratching his gills, "I guess that's settled then. We can't eat you, so what are we going to do with you?"

"Maybe you could help us instead," Amanda suggested. "You see, our space-egg has broken down and we're trying to get home to Earth. We've just been visiting our friend Skelly on Laktose and…"

"*You're friends of Captain Skelly?* Why didn't you say so – any friend of Skelly's is a friend of ours," said the Captain, as he held out a flipper and helped the dazed pair from their space-egg. "Welcome aboard the deep space trawler that goes by the name of *THE STARFISH*. I'm Captain Mudd Skipper and this is me crew…"

"Your name's Mudd?" asked Amanda.

"Always has been, ever since I was a small fry. Anyhow, as I was saying, this is me crew: Big Mack, Guppy, Kipper, Sharkey, Monk, Jack, Bubbles, and our longest serving shipmate Old Trout."

"Gosh! There's not many fish… er… men considering that this is such a large ship," said Amanda.

"We don't need too many in the crew 'cause most of the ship is used for storing scrap metal," Captain Mudd informed her.

The Captain went on to explain that they were space fishermen – that is to say: fish… er… men, because they were neither one nor the other. He and his hardy crew had been trawling the universe for debris, as it was their job to clear away dumped spacecraft and rockets which were littering flight paths throughout space. Apparently, abandoned spacecraft from many planets, including Earth, always ended up floating perilously around the Waste of Space – which was exactly where they were right at that present time – so any hazards or obstructions had to be cleared away. *THE STARFISH* was actually a giant vacuum cleaner which sucked up unwanted junk before crushing it, but any debris that was of salvageable interest was hauled on board by one of several trailing magnets trawling behind the spaceship.

After his explanations were over, Captain Mudd Skipper personally worked on the space-egg as he tried to find the fault that had caused it to break down. And, very soon, he had the matter dealt with.

"Used to work on these things when I were a youngster doing youth experience on Laktose," said the Captain. "Space-eggs are collectors' items now, you know. It's not very often they goes wrong, but they're a bit outdated these days."

"Skelly did offer us a new one," Amanda told him.

"Should've snapped his hand off," he said. "Never mind, this thing will get you home but, after that, I'd put it in a museum if I was you. Anyhow, I thought it was something simple that had caused it to malfunction – and it was…"

Captain Mudd Skipper paused to hold up a carrot in his flippery hand, and wave it in front of Amanda and Boggles.

"Here is the offending article," he announced.

Immediately, Boggles' little pink face began to turn a deep shade of crimson.

"It had dropped into the electrics and shorted the main power supply," the Captain informed Amanda.

"Whoops!" squeaked Boggles. "It could have happened to anyone, though – Sorry!"

"No... it could only have happened to you," said Amanda. "Anyway, accidents happen, so you're forgiven. It's not really your fault."

"With no power supply, you were lucky that you only caught the edge of the storm," continued Captain Skipper.

"What storm?" Amanda asked.

"The one that swept you into the Waste of Space, of course."

"I thought it was a black hole," said Amanda in surprise.

"If it had been a black hole you wouldn't be here right now."

"But the space-egg's displays were telling us that it was the black hole through which we needed to return," said Amanda.

"That's because it was malfunctioning. The computer must have been doing all sorts of funny things as it was trying to pinpoint wherever you where, so the first dark mass it picked up was the eye of the storm. It's working perfectly now, mind you – so, when you're ready, you can go home."

"Thank you so much for all of your help," said Amanda. "We can't pay you for the work you've done though, Captain."

"We don't need money; it's not valid in our world," said Captain Skipper with a big grin on his face. "Besides, you've done enough to help us already."

"What do you mean?" was Amanda's puzzled reply.

"Well, we've been at sea – sorry, in space – for a long time and we couldn't get home before now because our planet lies on the other side of the Milky Way. However, we had recently received the news that you and little Boggles helped to restore the beacon which illuminates the treacherous path across the Milky Way, so we too can finally return to our homes."

"Then it appears there's a happy ending for everyone," said Amanda with a huge smile on her face.

"It certainly seems to be that way," agreed Captain Skipper.

"Before you go though, I've been dying to mention the sticking-plaster on your chin," said the Captain.

"Everyone does," said Amanda. "It's a big talking point, so to speak."

"And it's useful for understanding languages too," replied the Captain. "Look, I've got one as well!"

Having made this statement, Captain Mudd Skipper pulled back the scales on his chin to reveal a sticking-plaster just like Amanda's.

"But... How? Oh, I see! So you're the friend of Skelly's who invented it! Well, I never would have guessed."

"Told you that I knew him," winked Captain Skipper. "Anyhow, have a safe journey home both of you."

"You too, Captain Mudd. Thanks for everything... Come on Boggles – Let's go home now."

A short while later, Amanda and Boggles resumed their journey, this time on their correct flight path. Once they were safely in motion, Amanda switched on the new transmitter and sent a message to her father. Then she turned on the space-egg's in-flight cameras and satellite tracking systems. Meanwhile, Boggles was becoming fidgety.

"What's the matter now?" asked Amanda despairingly. "Have you got ants in your pants?"

"You know I don't wear pants," Boggles cheekily replied.

"Maybe you should – It might trap in some of that foul-smelling wind of yours!"

Boggles ignored that remark.

"I'm looking for my carrots," he said. "You were supposed to stock up."

"I told you to lay off the carrots, at least until we get home. If nothing else, it may give me a chance to breathe better."

"But I need a carrot... *Like now!*"

At that moment it suddenly dawned on Amanda exactly what Boggles' problem really was.

"Oh, my gosh!" she exclaimed. "That's it, isn't it? You're a carrot addict – you're addicted to the darned things, aren't you?"

Naturally, Boggles denied this.

"No, I'm not," he indignantly replied. "I can easily live without them."

"Then why are you twitching then?"

"I'm not twitching – It's nerves! Yes, that's what it is, nerves... You know I hate flying."

But before the argument could become more heated they were unexpectedly interrupted.

"Amanda? Is that you?" said a familiar-sounding voice which suddenly burst over the transmitter.

"*DAD?* " Amanda shrieked. "Hi Dad – it's great to hear your voice... How are you?"

"I'm fine... More to the point though, how are you?"

Boggles was fidgeting around worse than ever now.

"Oh, I give up," Amanda surrendered. "Your carrots are in the glove-box, okay?"

Without hesitation, Boggles hurriedly opened the glove-box and helped himself. He immediately crammed a whole carrot into his mouth, which made his cheeks bulge outwards. Then he began to coo in a satisfied manner.

"Amanda? Are you alright?" came her father's voice again.

"Sorry Dad... Yes, I'm absolutely fine, thank you."

"Are you sure? It sounded as if you were talking to yourself. I hope that you haven''t developed a bout of space madness."

"No, honestly, I'm okay. I was talking to Boggles actually – He's the one with the problem."

"Boggles? You mean you've found him then... So, he's still alive."

"He won't be if he continues the way he's going!" Amanda retorted. "Honestly, he can be a pain in the neck at times, and I think he's become a carrot addict. He was shaking like a leaf just a moment ago but now that he's eaten a carrot he appears to be miraculously cured."

"Hmmm... It sounds like a bad case of Carrot Crunchers' Syndrome to me," said Dad. "Don't worry though, it's not incurable. Let him have his carrots, otherwise he will suffer from serious withdrawal symptoms and start eating the upholstery. We'll sort him out when you get back... I assume that's what you're doing, coming home?"

"We're on our way home right now. Turn on your monitors so that I can see you."

Amanda's father switched on the monitors in the control room at that precise moment, whereupon Amanda's space-egg monitor instantly flickered to life as it too became activated. Then she could see her father peering anxiously into the screen, surrounded by his team of scientists.

"Hi Dad… hello Ben, hello Mike, hi Alf," said Amanda. "Sorry, but I wasn't ignoring you, it was just that I hadn't realised you were all there as well."

"Hello Amanda," chorused the team of scientists. "Nice to see you again."

Amanda reached forward and touched the screen of her monitor and, trying to hold back the tears, she said: "I've missed you so much."

"WHO?" asked her father and the scientists, together.

Amanda choked back her tears and began to laugh.

"Well, all of you, I suppose… but I actually meant that I've missed my dad."

"I've also missed you sweetheart," Dad said softly. "And Mum has missed you too, of course. We were so worried about you at first."

"What do you mean, at first? Didn't you miss me later as well?"

"No… I mean, yes, of course we did," Dad replied. "What I mean to say is that Skelly managed to transmit a message to us – it took a while to decode but, basically, it told us that you had arrived safely on Laktose and were having a ball."

"Actually, the ball was yesterday at the palace," Amanda joked. "I didn't realise Skelly had sent a message to you; he didn't tell me, the rascal."

"Yes, at least someone thought about putting our minds at rest," Dad made a point of saying. "Mum was beside herself with worry."

"How is Mum, by the way?"

"She's better now…"

"Has she been ill?" Amanda interrupted, panicking.

"No… I was actually going to say: she's better now that she's got over the initial shock of you flying off to Laktose. It took some explaining I can tell you. She wanted to call the police, the Army, the Air Force, NASA… just about everyone for that matter. What the heck were they going to do, I asked her? She even wanted to call the press but I said it was in our interests to keep the story out of the news. Imagine trying to explain the whole situation to them? Anyway, I managed to convince your mother and now she's sworn to secrecy… I had to knock her about a bit, mind you."

"*Oh, Dad!*" Amanda gasped, raising her hand toward her mouth in horror. "How could you?"

"I'm just kidding," laughed Dad. "Your mother is perfectly fine really. She's a good person, you know."

"I know," said Amanda, letting out a sigh of relief. "Where is she now? I'd love to hear her voice."

"Er… That could be a bit of a problem," said Dad in a serious tone of voice. "You see, we had a spare full-size space-egg and your mother said that if a child could fly one, then so could she, and she's gone looking for you. Now she's up there somewhere in space – lost! Nobody knows where she is."

"Oh, my gosh!" Amanda gasped again, this time raising both hands to her mouth.

"Take no notice of him, darling," interrupted the welcoming sound of her mother's voice. "You know your father – ever the joker. He thinks he's so funny."

"*MUMMY!*" Amanda shrieked joyfully, as her mother's smiling face suddenly appeared on the space-egg's auxiliary screen. "So, where are you really?"

"I'm at home. Your dad rigged up a monitor here, connected to the lab, just in case you reappeared in the middle of the night when he wasn't at work."

"I'm so glad you're alright Mum. Dad had me worried for a moment, but I should have known him better. I've missed you so much... I've got a special present to give you when I get back."

"You shouldn't have."

"Oh, it's only a little something, but I think you'll like it."

"I'm sure I will... What is it?"

"It's supposed to be a surprise, but I'll tell you anyway. It's a box of candies – buttermilk cream flavour actually – and I've got several sticks of Laktosian rock for you also."

"Seems like a fair swap to me," Amanda's father said.

"Don't interrupt me, Bill; I'm trying to have a serious conversation with our daughter."

"Sorry my dear," mumbled Amanda's father.

"Mmm! Sounds delicious," Mum went on. "I can't wait to try it. And I can't wait to see you again either."

"Me neither," Amanda agreed.

"Well, you won't have to wait for long," Alf the scientist interrupted, "because Amanda is about to enter the Earth's outer stratosphere."

"Sorry Janet, we're going to have to cut you short," said her husband.

"Okay Bill… See you soon Amanda. Happy landings!"

"Thanks Mum… I love you."

"I love you too, darling."

Then Amanda's mother disappeared off-air.

"Put your safety harness on Amanda, and drop the sun visors or the glare from the sunlight will blind you," warned her father.

Amanda did as she was told.

"Are we nearly there yet?" asked Boggles in a sleepy voice. Having eaten all of his carrots he had felt quite content and then fallen asleep for a short while.

"Hang on a second Boggles, I'm trying to concentrate," said Amanda. "Belt-up now."

"There's no need to be so nasty," squeaked a pathetic little voice. "I was only asking."

"No, you daft creature! I mean, belt-up – put your seat belt on, we're coming in to land."

"Oh, silly me," chuckled Boggles. "I misunderstood you for a moment."

"Now there's a surprise," muttered Amanda.

With a crackling sound, caused by atmospheric interference, her father's voice then came over the radio again.

"Okay, Amanda – stand by. Communications silent for the landing procedure…We're bringing you home."

And that's exactly what the scientists did. Within seconds of Dad's last announcement Amanda and Boggles had safely touched down in the Room of Interstellar Activity, which was a welcome relief to everyone concerned. There were tears of joy all around when Amanda stepped from the space-egg, and there was so much to tell everyone too. Dad was over the moon at getting both of the space-eggs back intact because, although he knew that Boggles was returning to Earth, he had not realised that so too was the miniature space-egg.

A short while later Amanda arrived back at her home in Darwood to be greeted by the warmest of receptions from her mother, before being re-united with Tabs and Milkstar. Once again, her life was back to normal – for the time being at least.

CHAPTER FIFTEEN

Miss Throwpee Suddenly Becomes Cool

"…And that's about it really!" Amanda concluded.

There was a contented silence in the classroom.

"I said: that's it, Miss," Amanda repeated. "That's the end of my summer adventure."

"Such a shame that it has to end so soon," mumbled her form teacher in a faraway voice.

"But it's half-past four in the afternoon," Amanda announced.

Everyone at Sherbourne Hills Refectory School had now gone home for the evening. Everyone, that is, except for the pupils of Form VI and their teacher Miss Anne Throwpee. They had been so engrossed in Amanda's compelling tale that time had passed by unnoticed.

"Good Gracious Me!" said Miss Throwpee, almost falling off her chair. "Is it really that hour of the day already? How time flies when you're enjoying yourself, children… Children? Wake up!"

Then Miss Throwpee clapped her hands twice in quick succession in order to get her pupils' attention, for they too had fallen into a dreamlike trance.

"Wow! What a story," exclaimed Jenny.

"I never knew about your secret lifestyle Amanda, and I'm supposed to be your best friend," said Clare. She sounded a little disappointed.

"Sorry Clare, but I couldn't tell anybody about it until my dad told me that I could," Amanda apologised.

"It sounded a bit far-fetched to me at times," said Miss Throwpee, "but I have to agree with Jenny – it really was a great story."

"So you don't believe the story, Miss?" asked Jim Smith.

"I didn't exactly say that…" Miss Throwpee began; however, she was quickly interrupted.

"I believe you Amanda," said Terence Bull in earnest.

"And I believe you too," the remainder of the class chimed in at once.

"Thank you," said Amanda.

Miss Throwpee glanced around the classroom at the children. They had all gone silent and there was a look of worried anticipation on their faces, as if they were waiting for her to say something – something important perhaps.

"Well… of course I believe her. It was just difficult for me to admit it, I guess," she finally said, and it turned out that Miss Throwpee had said the right thing.

"Hooray for Miss T," bellowed the children. "And hooray for Amanda."

"Thanks again," said Amanda, reddening slightly with all of the attention she was receiving.

"Miss T?" questioned the form teacher with a serious frown upon her face.

The classroom went quiet again. Now that they had upset their teacher the children knew they would have to face her wrath.

"Yes, that's what we call you, usually out of earshot," Amanda owned up in a quiet voice.

"Hmm... Miss T, eh? It's got quite a ring to it. Yes, I like that... From now on children, you may call me Miss T to my face if you wish."

The entire classroom erupted again, just as if a huge explosion had taken place, when everybody cheered loudly.

"You're pretty cool Miss T," Terence Bull shouted, trying to make himself heard above the din.

"Why, thank you Terence," said Miss Throwpee, taking off her spectacles and grinning from ear to ear. Then she replaced her glasses and recomposed herself.

"Come along now children," she said. "It's nearly five o'clock, so it's time you all went home."

"Oh, Miss! Can't we stay a little bit longer and ask Amanda some questions?" asked Clare.

"No Clare – you will all miss the school bus if we stay any longer."

"We've already missed the bus," Terrence pointed out.

After a quick glance at the bus timetable posted on a nearby wall, Miss Throwpee realised that what Terrence had said was correct.

"Oh, so you have," she agreed. "Well, no matter, you'll still have to go home now because your parents will be worried about each of you."

There was an exchange of puzzled glances amongst the classmates when they heard this.

"SO WHAT?" they chanted together, shrugging their shoulders at the same instance.

Miss Throwpee took a moment to think before saying anything further.

"Okay, you win," she said. "Just another half-an-hour then – and that's all. I'll personally take you all home in the school minibus and explain to your parents the reason for being late home."

"Can you drive the minibus, Miss Throw… er, Miss T?" enquired Amanda.

"I don't know yet. We'll find out in a while though, won't we?"

So, Form VI got to stay on at school for another half-an-hour (which actually developed into a full hour) and, afterwards, Miss Throwpee was true to her word because she drove the children home in the school minibus, dropping them off at their front doors one by one. And she did quite well really, considering that she had never driven such a large vehicle before. In fact, she only managed to knock over three signposts, squash six litterbins, demolish a garden fence and bump into two parked cars! Actually, it was a miracle that anyone got home at all, as well as being extremely fortunate that nobody else saw her little mishaps; but the children were highly unlikely to tell anyone about it because she was now 'Miss T' to them and pretty cool in their books.

Amanda was the last person to be dropped off at home. She was about to step off the minibus when she saw Miss

Throwpee take a cigarette from her packet and put it into her mouth.

"You know, Miss Throwpee," said Amanda, "I don't want to interfere, but I noticed that you haven't smoked a single cigarette since this morning. You smell so much nicer now – maybe it's time you thought about giving it up."

Miss Throwpee looked thoughtfully at Amanda. Then she tilted her half-spectacles down a little and gave her reply.

"You know, Amanda, I don't mind you interfering at all. You're right – maybe it is time that I gave up smoking."

Having said that, she took the cigarette from between her lips, put it back into the packet and returned the pack to the inside pocket of her jacket.

"I'll keep them in here," she said, patting the packet with her hand, "…Just in case."

Then she smiled warmly at Amanda.

"What a great story you told today young lady, and well worthy of the top marks that I shall be giving you… Goodnight Amanda."

Amanda returned the smile.

"Goodnight Miss Throwpee," she said. "See you soon."

NOT QUITE THE END... AGAIN!

(Well, almost folks; however, there are still a few loose ends to tie up.)

CHAPTER SIXTEEN

The Last Bit

You may be wondering what happened to Boggles. Well, it turned out that he had indeed got a bad case of Carrot Crunchers' Syndrome and, after a week of detoxing, he was completely cured. He has never touched a single carrot since that day – quite a few bunches, but never a single carrot!

After learning that his favourite lab rat was afraid of flying, Amanda's father was a little annoyed to begin with, considering the time and money that had been invested in him. Boggles was therefore retired from service, thus making him homeless. But Boggles was still his favourite lab rat, so Amanda's dad brought him home to live with the James family, where he still likes to moan and wimp-out.

Miss T did manage to give up smoking cigarettes – and now she smokes evil-smelling cigars instead!

As for the fate of the escaped Rottanegs: they were not rounded up by an Inter-Galactic Space Cruiser Patrol at all. In fact, it was *THE STARFISH* that picked them up – literally! Captain Mudd Skipper and his crew were trawling the Waste of Space on the final leg of their journey home when their giant vacuum sucked the grotesque trio up the hoover. There they remained undiscovered for several weeks whilst refuse gradually piled up on top of them, because it was so difficult to tell them apart from the rest of the rubbish. It was only when a recycling machine was separating the trash that they were accidentally detected, for it apparently would not accept any old rubbish! The three rejects were then taken away and cast-off on a deserted planet for the rest of their days.

Meanwhile, back on Laktose a new fashion was all the rage. Having seen Amanda with the sticking-plaster permanently in place underneath her chin, many people had enquired about it. Amanda had become so fed-up with trying to find a different excuse for wearing the plaster that she had finally decided to use the same little white lie every time: "It's a fashion accessory," she told the people of Laktose – and that's exactly what it had later become. Every single person on Laktose who wanted to be someone now wore a Band-Aid upon their chin. It was now possible to get them in luminous green, pink, yellow, orange, and just about every colour under the rainbow too. They were also available as multi-coloured, tartan, see-thru, glow-in-the-dark, and even flashing neon lights – the range was endless. If only Amanda knew what she had started!

One of the first things Amanda had done when she returned home was fill in the missing planets from her star chart and all of the details that she could not possibly have known about prior to her voyage to the Milky Way. Whenever she had the opportunity, Amanda went with her father to his laboratory and took a peek at Laktose through One-Eyed Jack. And each time the planet twinkled she realised that there was a big party taking place where the Laktosian people were busily gulping down large amounts of the various shades of coloured milkshakes whilst they danced.

Amanda was much more settled now that she had seen Skelly again and she felt far happier with the knowledge that he would be visiting her on Earth again in the very near future... Just as we all know that he will surely return again one day.

STILL NOT THE END

(Except for the past and the present, because the future has yet to come...)

Look out for these other amazing titles by Wolfren Riverstick

The Incredible Adventures of Amanda and SKELLY   (ISBN 9780955431418)

When Amanda James moves from her home in the city to live in the countryside she feels extremely lonely at first. However, she soon befriends a creature known as 'Skelly' who has been stranded on Earth since crashing his space-egg, after accidentally departing from his home planet of Laktose in the distant galaxy of the Milky Way. This is just the beginning of a series of remarkable adventures between these two new friends.

A Cat Called Ian   (ISBN 9780955431401)

When a young boy decides to climb the magnificent oak tree on top of Sunrise Hill he discovers that there is much more to it than first meets the eye. After mysteriously stumbling into the mystical world of Catland, the unruly ten-year-old is whisked into a courtroom where he is punished with the Sentence of Nine Lives in an attempt to make him change the error of his ways.

COMING SOON

While You Sleep… *The Dream Snatchers Cometh*

Have you ever wondered where your dreams and nightmares come from or where they go? Well, wonder no longer because all is revealed in this fascinating insight into the unknown world of sleep. Meet The Dremlocks, The Inkybyes, the Jackson family… and find out what you would never have guessed about hamsters!